Also by Lance C Wilson

Dark Side of the
ROCK

A POWERFUL AND FAST-MOVING NOVEL
THAT CASTS NEW LIGHT ON ONE OF
AUSTRALIA'S GREATEST MYSTERIES.

LANCE C WILSON

Printed and published by Kimberley Cottage Publishing.

This is a work of fiction. All the characters and events portrayed in this book are either fictitious or are used fictitiously.

National library of Australia
    Cataloguing-in-publication data:

    Author: Wilson, Lance C., 1945 - author.

    Title: The dark side of the rock / Lance C Wilson ;
    Moira Horrocks, editor.

    ISBN: 9780977550579 (paperback)

    Subjects: Detective and mystery stories, Australian.

    Other Authors/Contributors:
    Horrocks, Moira, editor.

    A823.4

Edited by Moira Horrocks
Book and cover design by Jo Grant

This is for three wonderful women
who make my books possible:
my wife Cynthia, Jo Grant and
Moira Horrocks.

ACKNOWLEDGEMENTS

I hope I have done justice to this story having been given the inspiration by a friend, Grant, a well-known helicopter pilot, who was told the story – by a grader driver some years ago – of a white woman living with Aboriginals. All my stories over the years have stemmed from the wonderful characters I have met on my many travels.

Special thanks to my graphic designer and confidante Jo Grant, who works long hours putting my books together; a true inspiration. Special thanks to my editor Moira Horrocks who turns my spelling mistakes and shocking grammar, into books.

Again, my sincere gratitude to the many outlets all over Australia for stocking my books. The stunning book cover is attributed to Alan Jennison, a talented photographer, who joined us in Arnhem Land in 2013, and delighted hundreds with his superb wildlife photography.

A special thank you to my wife Cynthia, not only for all her hard work and for cooking delicious buffalo roasts for our many guests in Arnhem Land, but for providing me with endless cups of coffee when I am writing. Thank you.

Lastly, sincere thanks to all my readers who send me the most inspiring emails; they bring so much joy to an author. Once again, thank you to everyone and I do hope you enjoy this story.

FOREWORD

I have no need to remind anyone in Australia and the world, of the remarkable story of a missing baby at Ayers Rock in central Australia in 1980; it enthralled the world and the media went into a frenzy.

Perhaps like many, I had not given the story much thought over the years but at the time, I was rather disturbed at the lack of any *real* evidence and subsequent conviction. It was perhaps the most disgraceful and shameful period in our media history.

The conviction and trial did not contain the mandatory three items required for a conviction of murder. There was no body, no murder weapon and more pertinently, no motive. The trial was based purely on circumstantial and scientific evidence of a highly suspect nature which in fact, turned out to be false.

Both those charged had no hope of achieving a fair trial in Australia thanks to the disgraceful conduct of the media circus, their wild reporting of ridiculous claims and its "kangaroo court" that convicted alleged criminals long before the trial.

It was only recently that a helicopter pilot informed me of the presence of a white woman living with a small group of Aboriginals. *Did the officials, all those years ago, ever consider this scenario?*

I hope you enjoy my fictitious slant on one of our greatest mysteries.

ONE

The chilling wind blasted across the desert as the first of the sun's rays crept across the landscape. Embers of a small campfire struggled to survive as several figures dozed fitfully in the warm, sandy shallow incline they had scooped the previous evening.

Nala was only fifteen and heavily pregnant. At the age of twelve, she had been "promised" to her elderly husband who had claimed her as his "wife". The small group of nomads consisted of two other women and three men, including that of her much older husband. One of the men was known as Jarra. Jarra had joined the group fairly recently, having turned up unexpectedly at the camp. After a much heated discussion, it was agreed that he could stay with the group.

After only a few days, Nala had noticed Jarra watching her every move and giving her looks that made her feel most uncomfortable. She endeavoured to stay close to the other women on their food-gathering expeditions.

Nala had slept with her husband several times but he was far more interested in her food-gathering capabilities than sexual liaisons. Her attempts at thwarting Jarra's blatant desire failed, when several months prior, her worst fears were realised. One night, she left the campfire to relieve herself in the nearby scrub; everyone else was asleep. Squatting behind a sand hill, Nala became aware that someone was behind her. Unable to stop him, Jarra forcefully pushed her forward, entered her from behind and thrust intensely and heavily until he came deep within her.

Nala lay in the sand terrified. Jarra disappeared as silently as he had crept up on her. If the others ever discovered what had taken place, she would no doubt have been blamed. Returning to the campfire that night, Nala was so worried that they might have been seen by one of her companions. Thankfully she learned later that Jarra slept on the fringes of the camp and that he was extremely careful when arriving and leaving.

Now, as Nala stretched languidly beneath the sun's rays

she looked around for Jarra. Her encounter with him had awakened within her, a strong longing for more. Never before had she experienced such depths of desire and although she knew it was risky, her craving far outweighed her fear of being caught. She also knew that it was *his* child she was soon to give birth to. Jarra was strong and well-built, unlike Nala's older husband. Nala also discovered that Jarra was having sexual relations with the other two women. Once, on an excursion gathering wild fruit, Nala had seen Jarra and one of the older women having sex; a look of utter ecstasy on her face. Nala smiled to herself as she had previously noticed the seductive glances they had been giving him and knew then that he was in fact mating with all three.

For several days now the nomads had been travelling east, far from their traditional hunting ground. This detour had been at Jarra's insistence; he wanted to find himself a wife and the other men had happily agreed. The group knew of several larger mobs living around the Ayers Rock area and it was here that they hoped to add another female to the group. It was vital to the group to keep the number of members growing; otherwise they would eventually cease to exist.

Gradually, everybody rose from their sleeping positions, gathered their few belongings and in silence, began walking in line, east, towards the large rock they knew existed two days walk away. All of them knew too, that white people would be there and they intended to give them a wide berth. Nala understood that many groups now lived in close proximity to white people but her group had deliberately avoided contact with them. Too many bad stories had been told of the negative treatment received by her people and so her group had made a conscious decision to continue living in their traditional country their way and well away from the newcomers.

As the sun rose higher and the heat started to cloud the land, they stopped at midday by a spring which was hidden in a rocky crevice. There they drank thirstily their fill of the icy cool water. Jarra had previously speared a kangaroo – he was an excellent hunter – which was tossed onto the fire they had made. They ate hungrily and quietly.

Nala had heard that Jarra had been banished from his

own people because of his inability to leave other men's women alone. She was afraid he would suffer the same fate with her mob and she noticed how the other men appeared to keep their distance, begrudgingly tolerating his presence. No doubt they already suspected his behaviour towards their women and that is *why* they had agreed to travel east to other tribes, in order to try and find a woman for him.

Nala had never before been so far east of her desert country. Her family lived west of her present home and as with their tradition, had given her to her present husband on her birth as a "promised" wife. Jarra, too, had never been so far east, having arrived from the west out of the Great Sandy Desert; this was all new country to both Nala and Jarra.

The remaining members were excited at the prospect of reaching country that other tribes inhabited. A keen lookout was kept for signs of tribes they were familiar with who hunted within the area that they now crossed.

Nala often thought of her family that was now so far away. She came to terms with the knowledge that like many others, they had succumbed to the life of mission Aboriginals, travelling miles to Bidyadanga, and the La Grange Mission run by the Catholic Church on the coast of Western Australia. But as was the life of a nomad, she dwelt little on anything but the day-to-day survival of her small group. They were one of the last remnants of Aboriginal Australia choosing to live the nomadic lifestyle.

Nala had no idea that her group had once consisted of more than thirty but confrontation with white settlers had reduced the numbers to the remaining few survivors. The old men had avoided contact as much as possible with white people even though it was now two decades since the slaughter of their family and friends and all for the simple mistake of spearing cattle for food. As is with their culture, *anything* on their tribal lands that constituted food unfortunately was now not for the taking. They learnt the hard way that taking other people's cattle in order to feed themselves was wrong.

Now hundreds of miles from her tribal country, Nala blended into her small mob but as a newcomer, was rated little better than the camp dogs, particularly by the older women. They considered her useless and made her wait until everyone else had eaten before they let her chew the leftover bones and any remaining morsels.

Nala often caught Jarra glaring at her with his dark flashing eyes. He looked intimidating yet cut a fine figure with his lean, strong body exposing many tribal cuts. Since his arrival at the camp, tension followed his every move. She smelt trouble whenever he was around and the undisguised smouldering hatred of the other men was almost tangible.

Nala discovered that he slept on the fringes of the camp deliberately, noting every movement of the others, his shovel-nosed fighting spears always within reach. Even when he came to her, the first thing she noticed was the spears drop to the ground as he roughly positioned her, ready to satisfy his powerful lust. She knew better than to resist.

Spread out over the desert, slowly picking their way towards a large group of rocks, Nala was the first one to notice smoke rising from a campfire. Cautiously the group circled, and approaching from the south, stopped occasionally to scan the area. They came across a group of tents and cars. Quickly skirting the campers, the group moved into thicker cover towards a large rock guided by Nala's husband, who had informed the others, was only a short walk away.

Within her lore, Nala understood that although Jarra had taken up with her clan, he did not belong despite the other men begrudgingly agreeing. He'd never *really* been given permission by her husband; he had simply wandered into the land of another clan and expected to be accepted. In times past, this would have been considered an act of hostility and acted upon but because of the age and numbers of her small clan, he had imposed himself on her group and indeed herself, creating a festering hostility among the others with his presence.

Aboriginal lore was and still is an important and vital aspect of Aboriginal life although tragically it is fast disappearing. Thankfully it still exists in the smaller clans as they endeavour to remain outside the white influence. Ancient tribal ways receded into history as most of the Aborigines succumbed to the *easier* life on missions, cattle stations and large white towns. Dreamtime stories became largely forgotten as traditional beliefs and practices got pushed aside by the missionaries.

Nala's clan was now in unfamiliar territory although her husband and other elder members had visited several times before as a larger group. They had traded and participated in ceremonies but this had not occurred for quite some time. The Pitjantjatjara, who inhabited the Ayers Rock area and south into South Australia, roamed over an immense region in smaller clans and sub-tribes. No permanent settlement existed although a number of people lived around the rock in small groups and were supplied clothing and food by officials.

Little did the clan contemplate that their search for additional women would end in total rejection. Times had changed and no young female was going to willingly leave her family to enter the harsh life of a desert dweller. Clothing and white man's food had put an end to any young Aboriginal girl wanting to follow tradition and meekly accompany a much older man into a nomadic tribal life where her status was nothing more than a chattel;

the old nomadic life had ended.

On their second day, the clan approached a group of twenty or so Aborigines sitting around an old tin shed. Children played in the dust as the adults sipped tin mugs of tea. With formalities over, the clan of Nala was invited to sit down and damper and tea were passed around. Again, Jarra stood alone on the outside, his eyes darting everywhere while watching procedures; he was patently disappointed that there were no young females in the group, only older women and children. He gave them a look of disgust; they were clad in filthy rags and rubbish lay strewn everywhere. He also looked nervous as he glanced around; he was in foreign territory.

Nala too, decided to sit at the back and noticed how the others were talking about Jarra as he stood proudly against the magnificent backdrop of Ayers Rock, of which the locals had named, Uluru. Nala smiled secretly when she saw that Jarra was staring at her. Little did she know that the wily Jarra had more than good intentions towards her. He had already decided that if he were to stay or remain with Nala's clan, he would have to fight but understood that because of the behaviour of the other members, namely the males; he would be forced to either move on or run the risk of death.

On one-to-one he would win but with a number of combatants facing him he would be lucky to survive. Jarra deduced that pregnant Nala was his only chance of securing female company and in the short time of observing the others, concluded that the two older women would certainly not be leaving to head back to the desolate nomadic life. The men, like so many before them, would surrender to becoming fringe dwellers on the edge of white society.

Nala and her mob lived on the outskirts of the camp. One of the camp women, Alba, approached Nala holding a loose, billowy dress out to her. She helped Nala into it but Nala felt uncomfortable in the huge cloth that was far too big. Unsure as to what to do, she smiled and accepted the gift graciously. Alba fed and looked after Nala and she was the only one who would talk to her.

For several days Nala and her clan sat around enjoying the tasty food from desert pickings and in the evenings, everyone partook of a "liquid" that seemed to make them loud and argumentative. She was surprised to witness her older husband join in the drinking until he collapsed into a deep and heavy sleep.

After two days, Jarra disappeared back into the desert. During that time he had stalked the periphery of the camp like a boxer waiting in the ring for a fight; eyes blazing, waiting for his time to strike.

It wasn't long before Nala accepted the fact that her small clan had indeed surrendered to the convenience of camp life; being fed and clothed by well-meaning welfare workers. They showed no signs of leaving and settled into their new life by moving into a tin shelter among the other inhabitants who were already living near Uluru. Nala found her contact with the white social workers and tourists who camped near the rock a pleasant experience but she still remained wary when they approached; the terrible stories still clear in her mind.

Those who had decided to settle there already spoke the strange language of the white people and Nala began to learn several words by listening to her hosts and the white people who delivered food and blankets every few days.

Nala gradually felt herself slipping into the more convenient lifestyle, relishing the blankets that kept her warm at night and how she liked the sweet sugar and dark drink that was always available in a Billy on the fire. Now uncomfortably pregnant, a white bush nurse gave her an examination which initially alarmed poor Nala but she was immediately comforted by Alba who advised her that the nurse had powerful medicine which would help her when the time came for her to give birth. It troubled Nala that instead of following tradition by "going bush" to give birth, she would now have to go to a big building. It seemed at odds, even though Alba kept reassuring her that it was all "okay".

One evening, as the others sat around the fire drinking and shouting; Nala, tired and heavy with her coming child, grabbed her blanket and made her way into the surrounding scrub to find a safe and quiet place to sleep, away from the yelling and fighting she knew would follow. Finding a tree trunk, she lay the blanket down and as she did, a feeling of absolute terror overcame her as she caught the aroma of Jarra! Before she got a chance to turn around, he grabbed her and threw her heartlessly over the tree trunk, tearing her dress off at the same time. Harshly and blindly, he spread her legs and entered her from behind.

The pain was agonising as he rammed in and out of her, her belly ready to burst under his weight. She knew instinctively that her baby was severely damaged as the fresh, red blood flowed freely down her small, thin legs.

Like a wild animal, Jarra continued until he came, satiating his lust. As he withdrew, Nala rolled off the log and immediately curled up into the foetal position; the excruciating pain forewarning her that her baby was going to be born. She was too weak to walk the distance back to her friend Alba and looking up she saw the flashing eyes of her attacker standing above her, devoid of any compassion. Jarra picked up his spears and walked off into the night, leaving Nala writhing in pain in the red sand.

Alone and fearful of the unknown facing her, Nala crawled to her blanket and covered herself as she lay against the log. Huge waves of pain engulfed her, the sweat ran down her small face and the waters flushed from her mixed with blood. She felt faint and disorientated.

For hours Nala drifted in and out of consciousness, her frail body weakened by the blood loss and the fight to expel the baby already making its way out of her body. Hours passed and the new day dawned with still no relief for Nala until with one supreme effort she followed her instincts and pushed as the lifeless infant was finally born.

Lying in the shade of the tree as the sun heated the desert, Nala looked up in the haze above her and saw his blazing eyes. Jarra knelt down beside her offering her water. She gulped it down voraciously between gasping for breath and ate avidly of the food he provided her before slipping back into a semi coma.

Throughout the day Nala woke intermittently before being overcome with pain when she would then slip into unconsciousness. As the last of the sun's rays glided like a thief over the landscape, Nala struggled to her feet confused and unstable. She looked around for her baby and found no sign, her small breasts full of milk as her mothering instincts now surfaced. *Where was her baby?*

In the twilight, Nala tried to focus on her surroundings

and recall what had transpired since the attack by Jarra. It all seemed like a dream and then suddenly, in the still air, she heard a baby cry. She cocked her ears and in a trance, followed the sound silently and intuitively. She knew she had to get to her distressed infant.

TWO

Dr Keith Andrews sat in the heavy morning traffic on Sydney Harbour Bridge. Tired and run down, he had not had a holiday for several years. Married to Sarah, they had three children; two boys, Kevin, aged nine and Stanley, seven and an infant daughter Mary, who was only three weeks old.

The previous evening, the family had discussed going on holiday to central Australia and although everyone seemed enthusiastic enough, as is often the way, workload or family issues invariably arose to put an end to the idea.

Keith waited patiently for the traffic to move and in that time decided he would *definitely* inform his partner in their practice that he was taking a few weeks off and getting away from it all with his family. He admitted to himself that since the birth of Mary, Sarah and he seemed to have lost the spark of passion in their marriage; they were both invariably tired and just a little disillusioned.

Arriving at the surgery, the receptionist presented him with a cup of coffee and the first file of what was to be a long day. That evening, he also had two operations to perform at the hospital and knew that by the time he reached home he would be exhausted. Sipping the coffee, he placed the file on his desk and entered the office of his partner. He informed her immediately of his intended plans.

'Keith, I totally agree; you really need it! I can't understand why it's taken you so long,' said Dr Enid McShane enthusiastically.

'I know, I know. I usually have something planned but patients' interests or something always seems to crop up,' he replied tiredly.

'Okay, that's settled. We'll reschedule patients and why don't you and the family leave Saturday?' suggested Enid.

'Wow, so soon!' exclaimed Keith smiling.

'Let's not delay – just do it – agreed?' Enid shot back happily.

Keith returned to his office and before seeing the first patient of the day, phoned his wife Sarah, advising her of the decision.

Sarah was beside herself with excitement and in a rash decision, decided to keep her two sons home from school to help pack the family tent and provisions for the upcoming adventure. Sarah was rather unusual in that she had few friends and her behaviour could almost have been classed as "eccentric" to some. Since the birth of Mary, her sexual desires had somewhat cooled; in fact, she had lost interest in many things. Raising her three children was now all consuming and housework had put an end to outside activities. She'd met Keith at university and after a brief courtship, discovered she was pregnant. They'd married at once. Before they knew it, Sarah went on to have two more children, which resulted in her having to curtail her career.

Sarah and Keith had often talked about getting away and with a newfound sense of enthusiasm, Sarah and the boys began packing for the long drive to Australia's Red Centre and camping at Ayers Rock.

When Keith got home that evening, he was greeted by two rather eager children and a pile of camping gear in the front lounge. Sarah had dinner cooked and it felt like old times; the prospect of the trip had energised the family.

'I finish Friday at lunchtime,' Keith informed them over dinner.

'Shall we leave early Saturday?' Sarah asked happily.

'As this has been so spontaneous, let's head off on Friday when I get home and we can be well out of Sydney traffic by nightfall. We can stay in a caravan park somewhere,' smiled Keith, looking more relaxed than he had done in a long while.

After only a few weeks of marriage, Keith Andrews had had to face the fact that he had never been *truly* in love with Sarah. Yes, they were sexually compatible but unfortunately the relationship had cooled with the advent of children and it had simply become a commitment because of the children. In the last few years he had felt trapped in the relationship and had thrown himself into work; life had become routine and he hoped that the holiday might reignite their spark. How often he had contemplated divorce or separation but his relationship and love for his children kept him in the family fold.

In reality, the trip could be regarded as a honeymoon

because when Sarah had informed him that she was pregnant, they married immediately and then Keith continued at university with his medical degree. There had never been any discussion regarding their start to married life and the absence of a honeymoon.

Even this trip would be on a budget with the camping and cooking of family meals but behind all this, Sarah and Keith desperately hoped that the trip would bring them closer together.

They had both wanted to explore central Australia, particularly Uluru and so took great delight in poring over maps and planning their route from Sydney via the Mitchell Highway to Bourke and eventually Cloncurry; Mt Isa and into the Northern Territory, left at Three Ways, then onto the Stuart Highway to Uluru. As this was their first holiday, they decided to take a break of three months. They budgeted for this period and a return trip south to Port Augusta and the Barrier Highway. Because of space constraints in the family car they'd been forced to buy a small trailer to house the tent, cooking utensils and sleeping bags.

On the Friday, at about two o'clock, the Andrews family departed Sydney. Everyone chatted enthusiastically and little Mary, now a month old, slept peacefully in her secure baby seat.

Over the next ten days they followed a routine visiting all the outback towns and indeed found themselves bonding as a family unit. When they eventually arrived at the Uluru campground, they were worn out and so looking forward to a couple of weeks rest.

There were other families at the camp site who hailed from all parts of Australia and as children do, friendships were quickly formed.

On their second day, Sarah sat at the base of the giant monolith watching her two sons and husband as they wound their way up the track to the top of the rock. Although she felt content and happy, she too was aware that their marriage was not developing in the way it should and that the children were the only reason they were still together.

Sarah befriended some of the fellow campers but for some odd reason, Keith had become rather aloof and didn't join in as Sarah had hoped. Instead, he went off on walks on his own, completely abandoning her and the children. Their conversations struggled and Sarah felt isolated and alone. To compensate for this loneliness, she unwittingly reached out to others without realising that her own neediness was evident and off-putting. The poor woman was crying out for help.

She watched for some time as her two boys disappeared over the rim onto the top of the rock. She had to admit that Keith was a good, protective father to the children although she had initially questioned letting seven-year-old Stanley accompany them on the climb but Keith had insisted. She never took her eyes off them as they climbed higher and higher, noting how Keith held the younger child by the hand at all times.

Sarah walked back to camp to prepare the evening meal. A feeling of serene contentment embraced her and for the first time since meeting Keith, they were together as a family, away from work and enjoying a holiday, as a family. Sarah felt, in the sacred shadows of Uluru, a spiritual peace within herself. Looking around at the surrounds, the rock was changing colour ever so slowly as the sun continued its journey west; the stillness of the afternoon and the clear blue sky seemed a world away from Sydney.

Sarah was still pottering when Keith and the boys returned. Tired and thirsty, Keith prepared drinks for the trio while Sarah lay the sleeping Mary in the family tent. Watching her two boys playing with other children, Sarah chatted with a fellow traveller while Keith dozed on a chair he had placed in the shade of a shrub nearby. As evening approached, all was peaceful and calm. While checking on the evening meal, Sarah heard her baby girl begin to cry. It shattered the tranquil evening air but Sarah continued to busy herself with dinner, assuming that a feed and nappy change were all that was required.

Suddenly there was silence and, alarmed, Sarah made her way to the tent. As she neared the tent, a dingo could be seen disappearing into the scrub. Sarah ran hysterically to the tent and the night air was filled with her screams of disbelief. Mary was not in her cot. 'A dingo's taken Mary!' In the mayhem that followed, people came running from everywhere as they confronted a hysterical Sarah. A search began immediately, sweeping in a wide arc around the camp grounds, whilst others left to inform the local police and resort.

Darkness now blanketed the area and flashlights darted over the desert as numbers swelled on hearing the tragic news that swept the area in a short time. Sarah was sobbing and being consoled by fellow campers while Keith wandered around in a trance; unable to take in or even consider that such an event had taken place. Shock and disbelief followed everyone.

Constable Roger Hardwick, stationed at the resort, had been informed without delay and arrived within an hour of the disappearance. A police officer with many years' experience, he relished the quiet lifestyle of his station at Uluru. The incident was his first major incident in his career and although inexperienced in such an investigation, Roger Hardwick had one thing on his side; commonsense and a calm manner.

Constable Hardwick inspected the area and found many footprints around the tent entrance; he also noted that the baby had been removed without any great disturbance. Returning to the distraught parents, he and resort staff organised search teams to scour the area looking for any signs of the missing baby.

Roger took statements from as many present as possible including Sarah and Keith Andrews. Sarah was positive she had seen a dingo leaving the area with what appeared to be something in its mouth. His own experience with dingoes was that they usually only scavenged scraps from around the camp area and that if it *had* taken the baby, it would indeed be a rare occurrence.

All that long night search teams combed the area without success and even Hardwick admitted to himself that unless there was some other explanation, it would appear that a dingo *had* taken the infant. It never entered his mind that either parent could have had *anything* to do with the disappearance; it was just way beyond comprehension and belief.

Hardwick reported the shocking business to Alice Springs police headquarters. The search escalated as daylight broke and the officer in charge decided to send two detectives to the scene as the story had already ignited Australia-wide media coverage.

THREE

Detectives Antsy and Freeman arrived at Ayers Rock airstrip the following morning, amused at the already huge media contingent frantically running around interviewing anyone who wanted a few minutes of fame and all having their own take on the story; mostly basing it on innuendo and no hard facts.

Both detectives interviewed Sarah and Keith again along with several campers who had seen Sarah cooking the evening meal shortly before the discovery of the missing baby. It became apparent to the detectives that the chances of locating the infant alive had indeed diminished because of the time factor and the harshness of the terrain.

At this crucial stage, Sarah spoke to several of the media and through no fault of her own – simply because of her dress and demeanour – hardly galvanised any public sympathy. The mass of media, caught up in the greedy frenzy of trying to outdo each other and grab the best shots and story, put aside any sense of moral values and concern for the distressed parents. Outlandish stories and claims were hurriedly written and embellished with no foundation to base them on; just sheer greed.

The two detectives sat in the small cramped office of Constable Roger Hardwick, sipping coffee.

'Well, Roger, whadda ya think? Honestly,' asked Freeman sternly, a veteran of thirty years.

'Honestly? It's a bit of a mystery. Maybe a dingo *did* take the child and from what the parents say, I've got to go along with it as there's no evidence to dispute it,' Hardwick replied frowning.

'I agree,' Freeman replied nodding, 'no body, no murder weapon and no motive; three things required for any murder inquiry. I have to agree.'

Detective Antsy broke in, 'I agree it's a strange case but we have to go on evidence. Let's clean this up and get back to Alice, the bloody media are driving me crazy.'

That afternoon the detectives returned to Alice Springs

and handed in all their reports then resumed their routine of normal policing. Constable Hardwick assisted the shattered Andrews family who had been moved into a room at the resort. Although several more searches had been conducted, no sign or evidence of the missing Mary Andrews turned up; the child had simply vanished. The media interest did not diminish but intensified. The story was a worldwide phenomenon.

Fellow campers had packed the Andrews' trailer and belongings as they had decided to return to Sydney. Their journey home was long and sombre and to make matters worse, they were shocked and dismayed to be greeted by a large pack of rabid media wolves waiting to jump.

Again, Sarah confronted the media and again it must be said she did absolutely no good to her cause as a grieving mother. Too calm. No hysteria. Not the norm. Bias set in. During this period because of the immense public interest, wild unsubstantiated stories began to circulate, mainly dreamt up by journalists trying to keep a story that so enthralled the public. Some so sensational, they fuelled the bigots and zealots.

Not surprisingly, Sarah and Keith's relationship was affected dramatically by the tragic event. Keith returned to work but this also proved to be stressful as many former patients refused to bring children to him for consultation and it wasn't long before he recognised that he was destroying the once thriving practice that he and his partner had set up. It was mutually agreed to terminate the business partnership and Dr Keith Andrews became another statistic simply because of public perception and bias.

The behaviour of his partner in the practice had been another blow to Keith. Enid had been his first lover during their early years at medical college and it was during that time that the two young students had made a pact to set up in private practice once qualified. But life took over and they drifted apart. Keith then met Sarah and then married when she fell pregnant.

Enid was still single and her rebuff had cut him deeply. He was well aware of what he had to do in order to protect the practice; there was no other avenue open. Both agreed that in time, the door would always be open for him to return, although in reality they probably knew that was never going to eventuate.

Sarah had taken the news strangely he thought. Numbed by the loss of their precious daughter, she dutifully went through the motions of their day-to-day living, intent on raising the remaining two children and trying to protect them from the media storm still circling the family like a cyclone.

A few of Keith's medical colleagues, aware of their plight, arranged for him to work night shifts in the emergency department at one of the major hospitals and moved the family into housing in the gated grounds to protect them from the constant media harassment. This did little to stem the flow of media speculation leading up to the inquest.

Strangely enough, despite their circumstances and despite the effect it had on their relationship, they began sexual relations again to relieve tension and stress. They were alone, with many of their friends having abandoned them.

In the ensuing weeks, an inquest was scheduled for Darwin and on the advice from colleagues, Keith appointed a solicitor. Life became a waiting game. Sarah never wavered from the certainty that a dingo *had* taken the baby and saw no problem with the authorities stating to her few remaining friends and associates that no finding other than that a dingo had taken the baby, was possible.

FOUR

Nala stood still, almost invisible. In the twilight, drawn towards the soft crying of a baby, she stepped out of the bushes. Facing the direction of the tents, she walked quietly towards the cry and gently pulled the opening aside. In one swift movement, she swept the child into her arms and left as she had entered, walking into the growing darkness of the desert.

Returning quickly to her camp with the infant suckling at her small breast, Nala roughly removed the outer garment off the baby, cutting it with a sharp rock she had found nearby. Hurriedly kicking sand over it and picking up her blanket, Nala set off south to skirt the camp site of the white people. In her troubled mind she had found *her* baby and now her only quest was to return to her own country. Nala didn't like the fringe camp life of her people. Her small frame belied her inner strength and wrapping the blanket around the tiny infant against the night air; she looked west and strode off into the dark.

Nala only stopped once. Looking back she saw lights flashing far off in the night sky. Turning west, she focused on returning to *her* country. Nala knew she would be safe and relished the peace of her nomadic life. The drinking and boredom of fringe dwellers had not been a happy experience for her. She was so used to the nomadic lifestyle and had not adapted and never felt safe in the presence of white people. She knew that she had to return.

Aware it would be a long trek this did not deter her and with her "child" safely tucked in her small arms, Nala's newfound energy, coupled with her newfound maternal instincts carried her forward. Her austere life as a nomad and the traumatic experiences she had endured had toughened her for any further problems.

As she continued her struggle towards her familiar country, Nala, in her broken state, thought that her small mob would be waiting for her and so despite her pain-racked body, she persevered. After several hours, she finally stopped. Utterly spent, she hollowed out a small depression in the soil where she cradled her baby and covered them both with the one possession she carried – the blanket – and immediately fell into a deep sleep.

The sun was already beating down when Nala awoke. Her mouth was parched and the baby suckled on her empty breast. Sitting up, she removed the last of the clothing the infant wore which was already soiled and discarded it. Nala knew she had to find water and something to eat as she was desperate for sustenance.

Standing up weakly and taking in her surroundings, she recalled that to the west of her position water existed but that it was several hours away. Undaunted, she set off. It wasn't long before the baby started to cry, also hungry and thirsty but Nala staggered on; her little body running out of strength at every step.

Stopping beneath the flimsy shade of a tree, she peered in all directions trying to locate the water source she knew was nearby. Thankfully she eventually spotted the spring; it had been the water source they had used on the inbound journey a couple of weeks ago. She gathered up the whimpering infant and headed in the direction of where she hoped was the water; the midday heat burning savagely.

She was right. Upon reaching the water, she thirstily gulped several mouthfuls. It was so rejuvenating and after splashing herself and the baby, Nala turned her attention to her next issue which was locating food. She lay the baby down in the relative cool of a large sandstone slope. Nala could then not believe her eyes when in the hazy distance, she saw Jarra carrying his spears and a large lizard. She smiled. Despite his treatment of her, Nala was glad and relieved to see him as she knew he would provide for her and the child.

Jarra stood before her, his eyes narrowing. Looking at the white infant, he frowned and appeared confused but Jarra was smart and now realised that he had Nala all to himself. Things had worked out well because Jarra knew that the remnant of the group would never leave Uluru. Without conversation he stepped forward to the water and drinking his fill, then ordered Nala to gather firewood. Once he got the fire started he threw the lizard onto it, watching east for any movement. Jarra was apprehensive, unsure if the white people would pursue them into the desert if they suspected that Nala had taken the child.

They ate hungrily in silence. Nala was happy that she could now share with Jarra and didn't have to wait for scraps from the older people as before. She noticed his eyes and knew that he would mount her and satiate his lust. She was still sore and tender from childbirth and Nala dreaded the encounter.

As she got up to make a bed for her and the child, she saw Jarra coming towards her; his member erect, his eyes narrowed. Nala lay on her back, dutifully opening her legs as Jarra mounted her. Breathing heavily, he pushed roughly into her causing Nala to scream in pain. He pounded away, quickly ejaculating and rolled off her as she curled once again into the foetal position, blood pouring down her legs.

Jarra looked bewildered as he picked up his spears and strode off into the darkness. Nala cradled the infant who was now sucking greedily on her small breasts. Pulling the blanket over her, Nala tried to fall asleep but it was impossible to ignore the pain.

Shards of daylight struck the red sandstone escarpment as Nala rose stiffly. Still sore, she left the sleeping baby and washed her small body where the blood had dried. As she gently bathed between her legs Nala whimpered; Jarra had damaged her with his brutal advances and she decided to stand up to him against any further intercourse.

He returned shortly after daybreak carrying a wallaby which he threw onto the fire. There was no conversation until both had had their fill. Jarra indicated to her it was time to leave. Nala picked up the baby and in her small but determined voice, remonstrated with Jarra over his selfish treatment of her. Jarra was surprised by such a dressing down and scowled menacingly but after the event, he left Nala alone for several days, time for her small body to properly heal.

Nala could not know that her horrific ordeal had in fact rendered her infertile and although they were both surprised in the weeks that followed, Nala never became pregnant again. Disappearing into the desert, the arrangement suited Nala and indeed satisfied the powerful Jarra. He provided for the small family as the infant slowly adapted to the life of her de facto parents.

After several weeks of travelling, the family reached

familiar territory several hundred kilometres from Ayers Rock. Nala's husband had forgotten about her as had the rest of the mob who had settled into a life of fringe dwellers around the resort area of Ayers Rock.

Jarra, being shrewd, was fully aware that because of his inability to leave other men's women alone, several shovel-nosed spears awaited either west or east of the rangeland they now occupied. But more significantly, Nala was in fact the first woman who had the ability to satisfy his sexual cravings. They settled into a peaceful existence with Jarra using his extreme hunting skills to feed his family and Nala repaying by offering herself to him whenever he needed her.

FIVE

K eith opened the white envelope and looking at Sarah, said quietly, 'It's from the solicitor, the inquest in Darwin is next week on Thursday.'

'I'll get someone to look after the boys; they certainly don't need any further upset,' she replied anxiously.

'Fine. Let's hope it ends soon and we can reach some sort of closure.'

Both were cognisant of the media attention this would cause and how they would be stalked and hunted day and night once they landed in Darwin. Every move and every word would be scrutinised and monitored by the hungry press hoping against hope to get the best deal.

Arriving at Darwin airport certainly was a harbinger of what the next few days would be like. A large crush of reporters dogged their every move and although advised by their legal representative *not* to talk to the press, Sarah felt the need to give interviews both inside and out of the courthouse because she had nothing to hide. Sadly there was no way Sarah was ever going to satisfy the biased lot who sat salivating watching the screen every night.

After a short hearing the magistrate delivered the only verdict possible; *the child had disappeared possibly due to the result of a dingo taking the child* and virtually left an open finding.

Instead of accepting the verdict, a large proportion of the population believed that Keith and Sarah Andrews *must* have had some part in the disappearance of the infant and the speculation, vicious and biased reporting continued even as the couple tried to return to some type of normality back in Sydney.

By now the strain on their relationship was starting to show and the constant intrusion into their lives and stalking by the media remained intense.

The Northern Territory Police came in for a great deal of ridicule over the handling of the case along with several so-called experts who refuted the possibility of a dingo taking the child.

Several months went by and to the shock of both

Sarah and Keith, police arrived at their unit with a warrant to seize the vehicle they'd used to travel to Ayers Rock. Behind the police were the media who filmed the whole event, having been tipped off by the police of the coming seizure.

Once again the media madness began reporting that a new investigation had opened due to fresh evidence, whereas in reality, there was none. The Northern Territory police and government had both been shown in adverse light and bowed to pressure from the media to open an alleged "new" investigation.

The new investigation was led by Darwin detectives to form a case based on circumstantial evidence to convince a jury of the guilt of one or both the Andrews, as to the murder of their child.

It is fair to say, and any decent individual will agree, that for either Keith or Sarah to have any sort of fair trial in Australia was impossible because of the unwarranted bias and lack of evidence. It is also well known that any individual who sits charged with an offence in the box is viewed by jury members as *guilty until proven innocent*. The coming brief of evidence being gathered was also the first in Australia to be based on circumstantial evidence, along with alleged scientific evidence later to be found to be false.

It is also fair to say that most individuals sitting as jury members are ignorant of what the law requires to convict an individual of certain crimes. As for murder, firstly there needs to be a body which is a fair assessment; however, recent convictions have occurred without this most crucial part of a murder conviction. Secondly, a motive is required. *Why did the accused want to kill the person, and thirdly, where is the murder weapon?*

One retired ex-police officer stated that it was immaterial if the individual was found guilty or not, as there was never any evidence to prove her guilt.

Despite all the stress and drama in their lives, Sarah discovered she was pregnant.

She had no chance whatsoever. Alleged expert witnesses gave "evidence" on many aspects of the case with the aim of convincing a jury of her guilt. This so-called evidence lacked any significant bearing on her case from the "expert witnesses" who were summed up by a former police officer of being "so vain and narrow-minded that they failed to contemplate that their opinion and judgment could be wrong".

Keith Andrews sat in the court stunned as the jury filed in and returned a verdict of "guilty" on his wife. For all her faults as a human being, he knew that Sarah and he were not guilty of this most heinous of crimes. As he watched his wife being led from the court to face a life term, he controlled the urge to throw up. He was allowed to speak to her before she left the court precincts.

'Keith, *we* know we're innocent. Look after our boys,' Sarah mumbled as she looked at him dazed and broken.

Still stunned he replied, 'I promise.'

Sarah was transferred to Fanny Bay Jail while Keith returned home to two sad and confused little boys.

The media baying and howling gradually slowed down as they had got what they wanted – a sensational story at no matter what cost.

But there were still many who were shocked and horrified at the outcome and initiated a campaign for justice for Sarah Andrews. This campaign was a tiny light of hope in a sea of bigotry and ignorance but Sarah was to spend many years behind bars before the matinee jacket removed from Mary was found at Ayers Rock.

SIX

Nala sat contentedly by the campfire watching her six-year-old daughter play with sticks in the sand nearby. They had just returned from a successful food foraging expedition and a large pile of various bush tucker sat in the coolamon nearby.

Watching a large caravan of camels drinking from the spring below, Nala waited patiently for Jarra; he'd left early that morning on a hunting trip. With the wet season upon them, he had recently been bringing home wild ducks that he had speared in the many billabongs. Flocks of birds circled above, swooping swiftly as one onto the crisp, clear spring below, ever aware of the hawks that circled above, waiting patiently for any careless individual to stray from the flock. The hawks would then dive down at great speed on the unsuspecting quarry.

The cave mouth where Nala sat was in a rise that gave

her a view for miles over the desert. She could hear the odd grunt of a camel, and the occasional rumble of thunder in the distance warned her of an approaching storm. Small breezes of cool air preceded the storm offering light relief from the unrelenting heat. Squinting into the distance, she smiled; she could see Jarra who was carrying two ducks dangling in his right hand. Tonight they would enjoy a good meal of wild duck and bush fruit. Nala threw more wood from the pile onto the fire which was situated just inside the cave and just inside enough to escape the deluge that began to pound the red earth. Nala called her daughter to come in out of the heavy rain. She had named her Arora – the Aboriginal name for cockatoo.

Strong winds began to hit the land as Jarra, glistening from the rain, rushed into the cave and sat down. Nala threw the plump ducks onto the fire as the storm raged around them. Arora sat with Jarra watching the meal cooking; no words necessary. The happy trio was now a close family group. How Nala would have loved to go further west to the coast and visit her family but Jarra knew the child would create a great deal of interest and he was uncertain as to the kind of reception *he* would receive. Nala never understood or thought anything of the child she was raising other than it was her own and Jarra never mentioned it, as he was in fact the one who had removed her dead child all those years ago.

While feasting on their meal of ducks, they had no idea that a cyclone had hit the coast and that the storm was actually the tail end of the cyclone. Nala was not to know too, that her parents had been moved to Broome as the community had been badly damaged by the storm.

Nala made herself comfortable next to the child and lay on her side watching Jarra as he sat quietly by the fire. She felt happy and at peace and looked down at her sleeping Arora. Not wanting to disturb her, Nala rose from her position and approached Jarra from behind. Placing her hand on his shoulders, she pulled him backwards towards her and swung her legs over him. Smiling, she looked deep into his hungry eyes and as she felt his penis stiffen against her, she slowly sat over it and the two of them bucked as recklessly as the turbulent storm outside. They were consumed by their passion for each other, satisfying their lust that existed only between them. Nala was an equal partner and after climaxing, fell off Jarra, crawled to her bed and within minutes was sound asleep.

Morning dawned and Nala awoke to absolute stillness. Jarra and Arora slept soundly. Placing some wood on the fire, she walked to the summit of the hill looking in all directions and sat on one of the rocks. Not a thing stirred; even the camels had left the spring and travelled deeper into the desert in search of the fresh picking and fresh water that the deluge would have brought. Wise to the seasons, the camels had followed the storm inland and would congregate in their hundreds giving birth and mating. She knew that the desert would bloom and it would be a time of plenty, time for them to return east and wander into her previous husband's country.

Turning, she saw Jarra. Strong and powerful, he had certainly met his match in the small and feisty Nala. She grinned as she watched his penis swing as he walked towards her. Last night had been erotic and Jarra was keen for more. Pushing her back over the rock she was sitting on, he entered her quickly, riding her like a raging bull.

Breathing heavily, he came in one mighty push as Nala clung to his hard, strong body, savouring the moment, smiling at the perspiring Jarra as he slipped from her, his passion depleted.

Following him back to the cave, Arora was sitting up rubbing her sleepy eyes and hungrily eating the remnants of last night's feast. In silence, Jarra picked up his spears, Nala picked up the coolamon and the three of them exited the cave and headed east, ambling slowly along as their ancestors had done for centuries. Next season, at the height of the dry, they would return to the spring and its supply of water when all else had dried up inland but for now, it was walkabout time.

For the next week, Nala's family collected an abundance of food along with meat speared by Jarra. Uncomplaining, Arora gathered bush tucker in terrain and country most white people would starve in within a few days. She was happy and content, learning the ways of Jarra and Nala that had been passed down over centuries of survival in one of the harshest regions in Australia.

****

For several years they travelled in this fashion across the land of their ancestors. During these years, they often spotted planes flying overhead and twice, heard that vehicles containing white people were coming from "a long distance". They simply melted into the landscape at Jarra's instructions.

From a distance, with her dark, tanned skin and tousled unwashed hair, Arora looked like an Aboriginal. It was her blue eyes and fair hair that distinguished her from what an observer might believe her parents.

As Arora grew, Nala saw that Jarra was beginning to show an interest in her. Now, in any *other* society this would have been frowned upon but to Nala it was natural, particularly as Jarra had informed her that Arora was not of his skin colour and therefore was not related to him. Poor Nala insisted that Arora was his child and was devastated and crushed when she learned that her own baby had been born dead. Despite her fragile mind, Nala steadfastly believed that Arora was her own until Jarra managed to convince her that she had taken a white baby. At the age of thirteen, Arora gave birth to her first child and over the next seven years, produced four more children.

The little band of nomads now travelled far more slowly but each year they still followed the seasons over their expanse of land. This would have continued except that one year, when returning east to the edge of their hunting grounds, the group froze. Situated next to one of their favourite camp sites sat two, small houses. Approaching carefully, they saw no signs of life and entering one of the unlocked buildings, discovered several beds and mattresses positioned haphazardly while cups and plates lay scattered on the floor.

Nala, Jarra and Arora had no way of knowing that under a government scheme to let Indigenous owners return to tribal lands, hundreds of homes had been built in Arnhem Land, other states and in isolated areas. In nearly all cases, those who did return, left within months as they were unable to readapt to the isolation and lack of services they missed in larger communities or white towns.

Initially suspicious, they camped at the small settlement for several weeks, enjoying the novelty of mattresses and shelter. The houses had been built near a spring and a large windmill that was still active. It pumped water to an overhead tank that both Jarra and Nala remembered from their time at Ayers Rock so they knew how to extract water from the taps.

The two women who had been part of Nala's original clan all those years ago, had applied for funding for the houses and with the help of welfare officers, had had their application approved. They'd only stayed a short time, along with an older male, before abandoning the site. Nala was also not to know that her husband, Cobra, had long since passed away; drink and poor food having taken their toll.

The buildings proved popular with the group and they returned each season for the next three years.

****

One day, when Arora and her children had gone looking for food, Nala and Jarra, now ageing, lay on an old mattress dozing in the sun. They were surprised suddenly by a vehicle that pulled up in front of them. Uncertain as to what to do, they watched as two women stepped out of the car, smiling. Nala and Jarra couldn't understand what they were saying and so nodded and smiled back.

The women went inside the two houses, hurriedly writing things down on a notepad while Jarra and Nala stood silently outside. It wasn't long before they jumped back into their car and drove off. They disappeared into the desert and the whole incident was soon forgotten as their lives continued forward.

SEVEN

Keith sat at his breakfast table reading the local news. Many long and slow years had passed since Sarah's conviction and his health had deteriorated between raising his two children and visiting Sarah in Darwin each fortnight, plus working with volunteers trying to get a retrial. Naturally, the stress had affected him deeply.

Sarah had given birth to another daughter while in jail and the authorities had allowed her to keep the infant with her until she was three years old. The little girl was now twelve and being looked after by her father.

Keith accepted that their marriage would never be the same since her imprisonment. Understandably, Sarah had changed dramatically. Both sons had completed college and left home, choosing to move to other states because of the stigma attached to their names by the self-righteous hypocrites who still pointed and stared at them after all the years.

Helping their daughter, Janice, prepare for school, the phone rang. Keith was most surprised to hear the voice of his lawyer informing him that the Darwin Supreme Court had agreed to reopen the case in view of new evidence; the finding of the matinee jacket and new forensic tests on the supposed foetal blood found in the vehicle.

Hugging his daughter tightly, he tried to explain to her what was transpiring; that her mother might at last be coming home. No sooner were the words out of his mouth when he regretted them. After all this time, coupled with huge disappointment, why build up any hope. Keith had become a pessimist, believing nothing he heard, read or was told. His trust in the establishment had evaporated years ago in the heat and bustle of a Darwin court.

He then phoned the prison and requested to speak to his wife if possible. The wardens, having heard the news release agreed and a tearful Sarah begged him not to come up until the hearing the following month.

'If this nightmare doesn't end soon Keith, I give up. I can't go on and any possible hope will have vanished,' she sobbed quietly.

Keith agreed, terrified that she would give up and although the time dragged painfully, several of his staunch friends and supporters visited Sarah, vowing to attend the hearing.

Finally, with the waiting game over, Keith, the boys and Janice, together with a small group of loyal supporters, boarded a plane in Sydney for the journey to Darwin. This time they were prepared for the greedy, vulgar press who hounded them until they were aboard. The flight only took four hours but it felt longer.

As expected, they were bombarded upon arrival but at this stage of the ordeal, Keith's loathing was evident. Some of the vultures had the decency to display sympathy but it was all too late.

Sitting in the gallery of the court with Janice and the other two boys, now young men, Keith waited for the judge. He glanced nervously at his poor wife who had aged far beyond her years. The judge entered and without hesitation, ordered the immediate release of Sarah Andrews and swiftly began to alert the court to the many discrepancies that had unfolded in the case.

Sitting in the court was Roger Hardwick, the ex-police constable from Ayers Rock who had been stationed there at the time of the incident. Hardwick had left the police force a few years later and now was a security officer in Darwin.

When the judge had dismissed the forensic evidence, Hardwick shook his head as it was well known that the forensics had been supplied by a woman who was having an illicit affair with the detective in charge of the case – a vicious bastard who was only after glory – assigned to convict Sarah Andrews. Hardwick, a fair and honest man, had never understood how a conviction had ever been handed down as there had not been *one shred* of evidence. The conviction had destroyed his belief in the judicial system. Hardwick, like many others, also knew that political pressure had forced the trial against the Andrews in order to placate public perception that Sarah and Keith *must* have had some involvement in the disappearance, and combined with the strong criticism from the public aimed at the Territory Police, Sarah Andrews had been convicted but not by any factual evidence.

Hardwick slipped out of court inconspicuously as the crowd clapped loudly and cheered; a long fight against injustice and a painfully slow legal system had finally ended! Everyone knew that no further action would be taken against Sarah Andrews; that her shocking ordeal was over as far as the system was concerned. But everyone was also obviously aware that her return to outside life would be a hard and harrowing challenge. One cannot even begin to imagine how years of incarceration would impact on an innocent person and Sarah Andrews would have the media in her shadow for the rest of her life. Eager to sustain the public's attention, some media, fickle as they are, changed tactics and vied for interviews with Sarah in her support.

The Andrews family returned to Sydney but as soon as the front door closed, Keith and Sarah knew that their relationship had been over for quite some time. They slept in separate rooms and within time, Sarah chose to leave Australia with Janice and begin a new life in America. They had no choice. Innuendo and speculation would have been a constant companion had she remained in Australia.

Keith left for Brisbane and joined a small practice, slipping into obscurity.

The saga never lost momentum and predictably, Hollywood turned the tragic tale into a film with Sarah played by one of the most lauded actors.

Despite Sarah's vindication, there are still people today who firmly believe that Sarah Andrews *did* have some involvement in the death of baby Mary; and this belief was deeply embedded by the media coverage at the time. Despite unsubstantiated reporting, lack of any evidence and no motive, the powerful influence of the media, day in and day out, swayed people's minds and opinions blindly. As one onlooker relayed much later, 'If the press say and report anything enough, then to some it becomes factual.'

Sarah and Keith eventually met new partners and life returned to some semblance of normality. Decades later, a new inquest returned the verdict that a dingo *had indeed* taken the baby. Sadly, even though this brought some closure to the victims, their lives had been forever damaged, tarnished and broken. Yet, their ability to move forward and start a new life is a credit to the great gift of humanity;

that the human spirit can survive the most traumatic experiences and eventually triumph.

No peace will ever exist on the planet when so much hatred and intolerance exists amongst us. *Why do we spend millions saving whales and billions on weapons to kill each other, when each year, twenty five million young children die of starvation; a blight on humanity.* The treatment of the Andrews family was sickening and appalling, highlighting the weakness of Australian society and its legal system at that time; it contradicted the underlying values of a legal system designed to protect us.

EIGHT

Nala and her mob sat watching the last of the wet season storm head west. Soon it would be time to return to the houses they had been using now for five seasons. Jarra, although still a fine looking specimen, was feeling his age and the two eldest children of Arora now did most of the hunting. For the last few weeks Jarra had been feeling unwell and although he had bush medicine, large scabs had appeared all over his body. Alarmingly, he had also stopped mating with the two women which was totally out of character for Jarra who was always so proud and strong.

Jarra was also vain and did not want the family to see him deteriorate. In his own mind he knew he was going to the after-life. During the day he didn't venture far from the campfire and his once sharp, wild eyes had lost their sparkle. He was also losing weight fast. Nala had put off heading east because of his inability to walk far.

One evening, Nala heard Jarra groaning in pain. In all her time with him, he had never complained or showed any sign of illness or weakness. As the soft red sun rose, Jarra staggered to his gnarled feet and passing his precious spears to his eldest son, did as his ancestors have done for centuries. He stood proudly looking round at his assembled family. He then turned and simply walked off into the desert; his time had come. Nala and Arora sat by the fire watching the once splendid warrior who had been such a strong leader of their small band for so long disappear into the desert; they both knew they would never see him again.

The young members of the family were confused as they watched him walk away. He had been their father, their teacher and he had made all the decisions. Now he was gone. Loud wails suddenly erupted from the group as Nala slashed her arms, blood streaming down as she inflicted tribal sorry cuts. For three days they remained at the camp and on the third day, Nala rose and without a word, led her mob off on their journey east as they had done for decades. The eldest son carried the spears and walked ahead.

Jarra struggled with every step. Pain tormented his entire body and his breathing was short and raspy. He was a proud man and wanted his family to remember him as the strong, virile hunter he had been. They must not see him die. It would bring shame. Despite his weakness for other men's women, Jarra had epitomised strength and virility and with his flashing eyes, had drawn attention whenever he strode into camp.

His long relationship with Nala had been extremely satisfying sexually and Jarra had been a good provider for her and Arora. Wearily, Jarra sank to his knees and with great difficulty, positioned himself sitting cross-legged. Raising his head to the sky, he sang his death song and by morning he had passed away, blending into the desert as the dingoes circled.

Without the figure of Jarra guiding them, the mob hunted and gathered food daily as they continued their journey east. They were late this season and the bounty of the last rains had already started to disappear but Arora's two eldest sons proved to have been good learners and each night returned with meat for the camp.

Weeks rolled into each other until they eventually arrived at the two familiar houses. Nala was so tired; being so late in the season, it had been a difficult journey. Arora, now thirty-five years of age and in her prime, had taken over as leader of the group. Although Nala was only forty-eight, their lifestyle had attributed to her premature ageing. Life in the desert is inhospitable and is a constant struggle to survive. With the departure of Jarra, she felt vulnerable and alone; Nala truly missed his presence.

A decision was made to remain at the houses for several weeks as they all needed the rest before embarking on the long journey back to their seasonal headquarters in the great, hot desert. In their second week, they were alarmed at the sight and sound of a large machine that was slowly making its way towards them. Nala had seen one before and simply sat waiting. Panicking, Arora and her children ran and disappeared into the scrub.

Arora and her five children crouched together and with wide eyes, watched the strange machine as it moved large amounts of sand. As it moved forward, it left behind it a track; a track much wider than any of the animal pads they'd ever seen and its roar was far different from other vehicles they'd seen white people travelling in. Arora looked at her children. Her two boys, now in their early twenties, stood majestically clutching their spears. Balun, the eldest, glanced at his mother while the younger, Magnu, stood defiantly in front of his three sisters, Akala, Jumi and the youngest, Younga.

The large beast came to a stop as it circled the area in front of the two houses and then headed back the way it had come. Watching intently, a short, stocky white man in shorts and hat, stopped the noise of the monster and stepped out of the driver seat. He approached Nala who was still sitting by the small fire.

Bill Strong had lived his entire life in the Alice Springs area working hard at odd jobs and saving his money to fulfill his dream of one day owning his own business. He had realised that dream and was now the proud owner of a grader, contracted to the government to grade isolated community roads. This was the first time he'd been so far east and had been surprised when given the job to grade an old road out to this small settlement because few, if any, knew of its existence.

With the engine now off, Bill grabbed his tucker bag as he intended to have lunch with the inhabitants. He had been reared among Aboriginal people and knew most of the languages. At one stage of his life, he had lived with an Aboriginal woman and had fathered a son who now worked with him driving a truck with supplies, fuel, and placing drainage pipes across the roads where needed.

Bill approached the small figure and was taken aback as she was naked apart from a small string belt. He noticed that there was no Billy of tea sitting on the fire.

Smiling, he sat down next to her and spotted her sorry cuts that were recent and still healing. He greeted her in English and when she didn't reply, repeated his greeting in one of the local dialects.

'Do you live here?' he asked. He was rewarded with her smile and reply.

'Yes, this is my country,' Nala answered pointing west.

'Do you want some bread and jam? I also have some tea,' he offered. Bill was curious; *surely she was not part of a small mob still living out west?*

Passing Nala some bread spread with butter and jam, Nala accepted it heartily. How tasty was the jam and memories of her time at Ayers Rock came flooding back. She couldn't wait for the sweet tea to boil. Feeling relaxed and at ease, her shrill voice sliced through the desert air as Arora and her children appeared from behind the shrub. Bill Strong watched in amazement as the group of two half-caste young men, spears at ready, came forward cautiously followed by three girls. Bill's mouth fell open as he stared at Arora, recognising immediately that she was white.

Bill passed around the loaf of bread spread with lashings of jam and each one tasted it and smiled and then wolfed down the sweet meal.

'Do you have cups?' he asked Nala, pointing to his own cup. She nodded and spoke to one of the younger girls who went into the house and returned with five cups. Bill poured in the hot tea and adding sugar, pointed out to them that it was hot and to wait until it cooled; even so, one of the boys stuck his finger in the cup and immediately pulled it out with a look of horror on his face! They all burst out laughing; the ice had been broken.

Bill was intrigued by this group of people. He had a hundred questions to ask them. It was obvious, that as none of them spoke English, they had indeed come out of the desert to rest at this particular spot where they had been able to remain anonymous. Then it struck him; *someone* must have known they'd been using these two houses because why had he been instructed to grade the road in? It was so far in from Ayers Rock and funds would not have been expended otherwise.

Turning to Nala, Bill asked her if he and his son could come back later and camp there for the night. He informed her that he had bully beef and food which he and his son would share.

Leaving his Billy on the fire and the remainder of his lunch for them to enjoy, Bill returned to his grader to continue back down the track, grading the opposite side. Bill was a man of few words and those who knew him regarded him a decent person, quiet and unassuming. He simply got on with life but at this moment, he was totally engrossed in what he thought he may have discovered.

Arora had told Bill that Nala was her mother but he knew that she was not albino but white. He was fascinated with Arora but knew that he would have to build up her confidence before embarking on any questions about her background. It was patently clear that the children were half-caste and that their father would have been Aboriginal. It was a mystery how they had gone unnoticed for so many years.

Trying to focus on his driving, Bill kept thinking about the little group he had left behind. Hours later, he came across his son Wayne, placing a culvert across the road. Bill then suddenly had a thought that hit him like a speeding train – the disappearance of Mary Andrews! A cold sweat broke out as the possibility of Nala having taken the child, hit him. He decided not to mention his take on who Arora could be.

Shutting down the grader and locking the cabin door, Bill walked towards his son. No father and son had a better relationship than these two. Bill was proud of his son; he was a good boy who worked hard and, under his father's guidance, already owned land in the Alice and was building a home with the help of his friends in his spare time. This time of year they contracted to do roadwork and worked seven days a week.

Wayne dropped a concrete pipe into the trench he had dug and as his father watched on, back-filled the trench expertly. Having finished the job, he parked the machine, locked it up and walking towards his father, knew by his expression that something had happened.

Bill filled his son in on what had transpired that morning.

Letting out a loud whistle, Wayne commented, 'Sheesh Dad, that sure is strange.' Wayne knew that his dad was right; a small group speaking no English and completely naked was a rare thing and he too was intrigued.

When Bill informed his son that the group had no food apart from bush food, the two men decided to hook up their caravan, load it with tinned and frozen food for an extended period from town and tow it to the settlement to share with the others.

NINE

Bill and Wayne set about packing the annex of the caravan and winding the stabiliser bars up in preparation for the move. They'd camped in the area for several days and were keen to make a move and enjoy some new company. Bill had not been able to get Nala and her mob out of his mind. *How had they managed to live beneath the radar for so long?* During all his travels to different communities, not once had there been any whisper of a white woman living as an Aboriginal. Apart from being fascinated by their story, Bill knew too, that he was attracted to Nala. He kept recalling her pert breasts and lean body and having been on his own for so long, had forgotten how much he missed the company of an attractive woman.

The old caravan, originally bought from a circus, had seen better years and while Bill had been building his modest home in Alice, it had been his temporary home.

Bill was a proud man and did not believe in borrowing money. Wayne had been born in the caravan so it was a huge part of his life. Some eight and a half metres long it boasted everything to make life comfortable; even a generator which he ran several hours a day to keep his freezer frozen. Over the years Bill had gradually updated its interior but had neglected the outside which belied its cosy and modern interior. Bill had his own bedroom and Wayne slept at the front of the caravan in a bunk with cupboards beneath. Every inch of space had been thoughtfully utilised making it a home-away-from-home during their extended periods in the bush.

It was dusk as they arrived at camp. Nala, Arora and the children stood up as they saw the truck and caravan but on recognising Bill and his son, they relaxed and sat down again around the campfire. A large lizard was cooking slowly over the coals.

Alighting from the vehicles, the two men set up the caravan while Nala and her mob watched in fascination. Having set up the annex, Bill then started the little generator and switched on an outside light which proved to be mesmerising to the onlookers.

Wayne sliced up some cold beef and placed it on plates with two slices of toast and a splashing of tomato sauce. He then proceeded to open cans of coke and passed one out to each of the youngsters, demonstrating how to drink from the cans. It wasn't long before Wayne was chatting away to Nala in her native dialect; the same dialect of his mother.

Wayne was instantly attracted to one of Arora's daughters; Akala. Akala was twenty-one and had the same sparkling eyes of her late father, Jarra. Even Bill admitted to his son that she was a rare beauty.

For three days Bill and Wayne remained with Nala's mob. The two men had worked non-stop for many weeks and decided to have a few days rest before returning to Ayers Rock where another project awaited them.

Wayne hunted with the two boys Magnu and Balun. He introduced them to a rifle and discovered they were quick learners; marvelling at the killing power of the noisy weapon.

Bill and Wayne carried alcohol but were loath to

introduce it to their guests as they were unsure as to how they would be affected.

On their second night, Bill, who had befriended Nala, took her to his bed and consummated their relationship. After showering, Nala was offered one of Bill's shirts to wear and with encouragement from Nala, Akala and Wayne also shared the same bed. In circumstances such as these, new relationships were established quickly and easily.

The two new relationships caused a dilemma for Bill and Wayne as naturally, neither wanted to leave their women behind but knew that Arora and her other children would be deeply distressed if Nala and Akala left with them. Bill also decided not to pursue his crazy thoughts about Arora's past as it would be far too risky for the vulnerable group. Introducing them to his society would require careful planning and diplomacy as he was conscious of their ancient culture and deep-rooted beliefs.

In a strange twist of events, lying in bed that evening, Bill was discussing with Nala his ideas and hopes and Nala, in her simplistic and naïve way, suggested that Bill take two wives. After all, as far as Nala was concerned, she now belonged to Bill. Jarra had taken two wives, so if Bill were to accept Arora as a second wife and Wayne were to accept the two daughters, then they could *all* move to Bill and Wayne's country. In Aboriginal culture, this bonding or staying together is known as the "kinship system".

Bill knew of a Kiwi living with three Aboriginal women at Pine Creek and the practice in Aboriginal society was widespread and accepted.

Initially Wayne seemed a little shocked with the idea but when they discussed it further and Akala and Arora seemed more than happy with the suggestion, Bill and Wayne agreed. Bill knew that if his relationship with Nala were to continue, he would have to take her to his home on a few acres of land, west of Alice Springs. There, he would slowly and gradually introduce her and Arora to modern society. He even had plans to involve the two boys in his business. To his thinking this was his only option. Wayne's house, on the adjoining block, was close enough for all five women to support each other yet isolated enough to avoid scrutiny. Bill realised that Arora would not create any interest there but remaining where they were, well-meaning welfare workers would soon intervene if they knew of her existence.

That evening, to the best of their ability and with much laughter, everyone took turns showering in the caravan and shared the spare clothes that Bill and Wayne had so generously brought with them. A decision was made to pack up, leave the van there and take both vehicles and all concerned into Alice Springs the following day. Bill's plan was to set them up in his house and buy new clothing for all of them. Bill knew that Nala would keep the other women at a low profile whilst he and Wayne, plus the two boys, Balun and Magnu, would return and finish the contract.

That evening, Wayne slept on a double mattress in one of the two houses together with his three women, while Bill slept with his two women in the caravan. Although a rather unusual scenario, the women seemed more than happy. The bush dwellers now knew that they would never return to the desert, that the two new men in their lives supplied plenty of food and soft beds and clothing to keep them warm in stark contrast to freezing desert nights sleeping uncomfortably next to a fire. Old ways are soon forgotten when life becomes easier and for the women in particular; intimacy was a vital element for without it, the human spirit is empty. All their needs were satisfied.

Rising early, the new day saw them squeezing into both vehicles amidst shrieks of laughter, coupled with excitement at the prospect of a new future. They headed off in the direction of Alice Springs and Bill and Wayne had many questions and points of interest to answer as they made their way past Uluru and Kings Canyon. The drive was long, broken by several stops and it was late in the afternoon when they finally reached Alice.

Wayne's home was within walking distance but as it was still unfinished, he and his three women slept on a spare bed whilst Bill, Arora and Nala bedded down in his room. The two young boys chose the spare room with mattresses on the floor.

Wayne drove into town that first evening and returned with a large bucket of Kentucky Fried chicken washed down with orange juice. The newcomers were quick to adapt and thoroughly enjoyed their "unusual" dinner. The novelty of switching on lights even became a game as it was all so different and thrilling. Despite their almost child-like fascination with Bill and Wayne's world, Bill knew how essential it was for them to be introduced and educated gradually as he had profound respect for their ancient culture. Too fast could be disastrous.

Bill took Nala to Kmart in Alice Springs and watched as she gaped in awe at everything. Fortunately it was early with only a few shoppers who watched amused, as Bill, clad only in shorts and boots, swept along the aisles with a tiny Aboriginal woman wearing a large shirt. What would their reactions have been if they knew that that was *all* she was wearing! Loaded up with random-sized women's panties, along with bras and dresses, Bill strode up to the checkout and placed them all in front of the rather bemused young girl at the till.

Once back home, the scene was hilarious as panties and bras were trialled and then swopped by the two inexperienced young men. The five women were lapping up all the attention and eventually delighted Bill with a parade; Bill beamed as he looked at the transformation.

In a few short days, they had gone from nakedness to pretty dresses and they looked wonderful!

Bill's handiwork had certainly paid off. Wayne's clothes fitted the young boys and the whole group looked pretty normal to an outsider; except for the lack of shoes.

The next big feat was for Bill and Wayne to take the girls with them into town to grocery shop. Nala had been relaying her expedition to Kmart and they were caught up in her enthusiasm and amazing tales. Bill suggested they go as a family as it would be their first encounter with the "modern" world. Before leaving, Bill warned everyone to keep together and not to wander off from the group. Alcohol in the town was an issue and when Bill tried to explain it to them they looked at each other and shrugged their shoulders. They had no idea of what he was trying to warn them of; how this white man's liquid could make one crazy. Driving into the centre of Alice Springs was, on its own, a big enough exploit as the newcomers stared in wonder at the traffic, the noise and when parking the vehicle in the car park, they clung to each other, unsure of the swirl of humanity who were too busy to even notice them; all absorbed in their own little worlds.

Once inside the supermarket, the mesmerised group gaped at the long rows of brightly coloured "things". They had no idea what they were looking at. Wayne and Bill grabbed a trolley and slowly wound their way down the aisles, pointing out to the little band of followers what each item was and gradually filling the trolleys with items they hoped Nala and the girls would like. Bill suggested to Wayne that they buy the healthier items as he knew that after a lifetime of bush tucker, some of the processed foods would not agree with their digestive system. Bill was so patient explaining each move as he led them up to the checkout where luckily, a part-Aboriginal woman picked up on the scenario and began to assist Bill as he placed the items on the counter. She was wonderful and explained how the system worked and even tried to educate them about money.

After loading everything into the two vehicles, Bill took them on a tour of Alice Springs and its surrounds. As Bill and Wayne drove across the Todd River, several Aboriginals staggered about drunk and this was the ideal opportunity for Bill and Wayne to alert the group to the negative effects of alcohol, how it could kill you if used to excess and the impact it has on one's life and family. Nala seemed to grasp this new knowledge which pleased Bill enormously. Nala, being the matriarch, would hopefully influence the others enough to keep them away from this temptation.

On the spur of the moment, Wayne pulled his father over and mentioned how he knew a part-Aboriginal girl who ran a hairdressing salon. Wayne thought that perhaps the women might like a haircut. At first, Nala frowned at the prospect of having her hair cut but Wayne pointed out other Aboriginal girls with nice hairdos and she relented, even smiling shyly at the idea.

Bill sat in his vehicle chatting to the two boys while the women were in the salon. He smiled to himself as he wondered how fate had brought him this new lease of life. Meeting Nala had given him a different direction. Wayne relished his new position; what man wouldn't! He now had three charming, good-looking nymphs waiting patiently each night to see who would be first to mate with their man. The women made love without reservation and whenever possible. Nala had rekindled Bill's sexual energy.

An hour later, the five women emerged from the salon beaming with their transformation which was amazing to Bill and Wayne! It was hard to believe that a little over a week ago, they were naked nomads. Arora in particular, made the biggest transition. Even after years of living in the desert and beneath the unrelenting sun, with her blonde hair now cut and shining, she looked a picture. She smiled at Bill and he shook his head in awe at his good fortune.

Now more than ever Bill knew he had to maintain the status quo. Somehow, he had to protect them and shelter them from scrutiny by the ever zealous welfare officers who patrolled the streets of Alice looking to pick up those Aboriginals who, because of white influence, were facing incessant associated problems.

Gradually, it began to dawn on Nala that meeting Bill and Wayne had been a godsend. She could not even begin to imagine how their lives would have been if welfare had picked them up and transferred them to one of the major towns. They would have been so lost in a new world without direction or guidance. Nala was oblivious to how the majority of the white society would disapprove of their lifestyle with Bill and Wayne but alleged experts to date have failed in resolving the problems with Indigenous Australia. That evening, Bill beckoned his son to the kitchen while their new family sat watching TV, staring and pointing at the big screen, enthralled.

'Son, we now have a *huge* responsibility and what we've done really worries me. We've seven innocent people here who trust us completely and yet we have to tread so carefully; how are we going to introduce and assimilate them into our dysfunctional society?' asked Bill solemnly.

'I know Dad, I follow what you say and I have to admit to feeling uncomfortable at sleeping with three innocent girls but the reality is, if we hadn't found them, their fate could have been much worse. I mean, look at all the communities we visit and in the towns where other Aboriginals are; do you really think these innocents would be better off thrown into that lot?' replied Wayne rhetorically.

Bill shook his head and replied, 'I have to agree, so what we need to do now is look after the whole family. I'm going to teach the boys how to drive the trucks and graders and then we can pay them so at least they'll have a trade. The last thing I want is for them to wander aimlessly like most and start drinking; they'd be so easily led.'

'Yeah, you're right Dad. I'm going into town to buy another caravan as I'm worried about leaving the women here. You and Nala and Arora can have your van, we'll pitch a tent for the boys and I'll live with the three girls in my new van,' said Wayne.

'Great idea Wayne and I'll help you with the money. While you're in town, stock up on enough food for at least two months. We'll finish the contract before we come home. We've several good spots to set up camp each time we move and we can teach them English every night!' Bill sounded relieved with his son's idea.

Wayne left immediately, taking the three girls with him. He'd made up his mind to let them accompany him at all times if possible – each venture introduced them one step closer to the new world they now faced. During their absence, Bill and the others packed his vehicle ready for the return trip. While they worked, Nala and Arora opened up about their past life. Bill learned about Ayers Rock and Jarra who had taken her from her promised husband. Everything Bill was hearing now seemed to fall into place but he decided to keep his counsel. He also tried to convince himself that it was in the best interest of all parties and just not his own carnal lust for the two women.

His whole life experience to date had taught Bill that the girls and Nala, because of their innocence, would be vulnerable if exposed to Indigenous communities. Beatings and rapes, drunkenness and a dysfunctional society would destroy them. His own wife, whom he'd adored and mother to his precious son, was unable to avoid the evil of alcohol and tragically it eventually killed her. When he had gone off to work with Wayne, Bill reflected somewhat guiltily that due to loneliness, she had taken refuge in the town and got involved in binge-drinking sessions. How often had he roamed the streets looking for her, only to find her beaten and filthy. Bill had pleaded with her, even begged her to accompany them on their trips but she steadfastly refused; the demon drink had possessed her soul like so many of her fellow countrymen.

Bill was now even more determined to shield his new family from the evils of drink and hopelessness that hung over Indigenous society like a heavy, dark cloud. Nala and her small group had indeed been lucky for inside Bill Strong beat a heart of gold and he had instilled the same values in his son.

Loading the last of the bags into the vehicle, Nala struggled to lift her bag of new possessions. Bill bent down to help her and looking into her sweet, smiling face, leaned over and kissed her gently. Nala drew back, a look of concern on her face. Bill pulled her towards him and explained that it was a sign of deep affection. Nala looked at him, tilted her head to one side and staring into his eyes, smiled. He knew she understood.

TEN

Sitting on the verandah waiting for Wayne to return, Bill began to worry. It had been several hours and he knew if they left now it would be well after midnight before they reached the camp. Since he had kissed Nala, he found her looking at him with a soft smile on her face. Her features were small and different from the local Aborigines and then it struck him; of course! Nala had Afghan blood in her like many who came from the western tribes; that explained her slight pointed nose and delicate features.

Bill was relieved and pleased when Wayne finally returned, pulling an eighteen foot caravan. He jumped out, sweat pouring off him.

'Sorry Dad', he exclaimed breathlessly, 'by the time I bought the van, transferred the rego which took two bloody hours, Jumi then had a "girl thing" – never thought about that – so went to the chemist for women's supplies.

I then went to Coles and we filled three trolleys and packed the van. Took longer than I thought and to be honest Dad, I am fiscally fucked and stuffed!'

'Okay Wayne,' chuckled Bill. 'Never thought of that either! Did you get some for Arora?'

'Yep Dad, spent a bloody fortune. Got some other supplies too from the chemist, thought we might need a few things,' replied Wayne looking hot and flustered.

Bill Strong was proud of his son. He'd always been a good planner who thought outside the square.

'What d'ya reckon if we leave now, and only go as far as the rest area before Kings Canyon this afternoon?' asked Bill.

'Yeah, that's good Dad, the sooner we get back to work the better, lost enough time now,' Wayne shot back and hopped into the vehicle.

The little convoy drove off heading west. Younga waved back happily at her mother Arora. Bill still struggled to believe what had transpired in such a short time. During the drive, he and Wayne had spent the time teaching their eager pupils as much English as possible. Pointing and translating took up a great part of the trip and it was all made a lot easier with both men having a decent grasp of their language. Laughter and giggling filled the air as the pupils all tried to outdo each other in pronouncing some of the complicated English versions.

Arriving at the camp site late that evening they found several caravans and motor homes already set up for the night. They pulled up together some distance from the rest and set about preparing the evening meal. Bill and Wayne still took the major role in cooking but Akala and Jumi were keen to prove themselves and pitched in. Large steaks were soon sizzling in the two frying pans along with tomatoes and vegetables.

Although Bill and Wayne often had a can of beer while tea was cooking, they had agreed to abstain and everyone drank lemonade. Several of their fellow campers walked past, many stopping for a chat. They were all older Australians and very friendly which was a positive introduction for the newcomers to white society. However, Bill knew that one day they would encounter the not-so friendly people and that played on his mind constantly.

Retiring to their respective caravans, Bill and Nala, followed by Arora, cuddled into the soft bed. Nala leaned over and kissed Bill gently. It then dawned on tough old Bill that he was in love with a tiny Aboriginal woman and also with Arora. He frowned at how this was possible but admitted to himself that he adored them both and swore he would take care of them until death parted them.

Waking early they enjoyed a breakfast of toast and sweet tea, before pulling out and leaving their older neighbours still sleeping. *Old age*, thought Bill, *has its rewards. After years of working hard and raising kids, the* grey nomads *as they'd been nicknamed, were now enjoying their last years touring Australia, and rightfully so.*

They reached the camping area at lunchtime. A decision had been made not to return to the houses where they had first encountered Nala and her family. They had their reasons, the main one being not to stir up memories of the settlement and also, only a couple of days' work remained before they had to move south to a new location. Setting up the camp well off the road in a nice quiet spot, Bill and Wayne knew that no one travelled this road. It was purely by chance as well as luck that the two health workers who had come across Jarra and Nala had requested the road be graded; otherwise they may never have found their new family.

Wayne and Magnu started the excavator and the task of learning. Balun went in the grader with Bill and the lessons began. The boys shocked their benefactors by taking to the task like ducks to water; they not only immediately started to grasp the basics but seemed to have a good feel for operating machinery.

The next few weeks saw the little band move from camp to camp repairing roads to isolated communities. Their new lives settled into a happy rhythm and no one appeared to be missing their former lifestyles. Magnu became a competent grader driver which freed up Bill to move the camp whilst work continued. Balun preferred driving the truck, loading it with gravel and spreading it for his brother. Each time they passed through communities, they visited the stores and stocked up on food. Magnu decided to try and apply for a licence for the fuel truck and proudly gave his name as, Magnu Strong.

Strong was then adopted as the family name.

English gradually became the preferred language, not because Bill demanded it but because he knew English would be the main language for the younger members when it came to things like applying for drivers' licences and shopping.

On one trip back to the camp, Nala had accompanied Magnu who proved himself to be a competent and trustworthy member of the small business. In fact, Magnu and Balun were paid in their second week! So competent and reliable, Bill decided to take over another grader and truck from an old friend who had several government contracts after a colleague had suffered a heart attack. The working force was now split in two with Wayne and the girls – who now drove the utes with the fuel and the caravan – and Balun, who assisted in moving camps.

Bill, helped by Magnu, ran the old plant/grader. They all worked together as a team but had their own allocated sections of road; but when it came to camping they remained together as one big, happy family.

Over the next six months, the younger members, at

Bill and Wayne's goading, obtained their drivers' licences. With each little step their confidence grew. Bill even taught Arora to drive the utes and she too obtained her licence. Nala unfortunately was too small to operate the vehicles but she was content and fulfilled with her little world and being loved by a doting Bill.

One day, while Magnu was driving with Nala next to him chatting, they noticed a girl sitting on the side of the isolated track. Her head was in her hands and she was alone. Magnu immediately pulled over and to their shock, saw that she had been badly beaten. Placing her in the truck, Magnu arrived back at camp with their unexpected "extra passenger". Nala was fussing as she was so concerned but unsure as to how such a thing could happen. Yes, Nala had experienced sex and knew not to protest but she had *never* been beaten. The poor girl had swelling and bleeding.

Bill set about cleaning her up; thanking the heavens that Wayne had had the foresight to buy that first-aid kit. When it had just been the two of them, they had travelled with very little, let alone a first-aid box. Bill gently gleaned from the young girl that she had been dumped and he guessed raped, after an altercation in a carload of reprobates returning from a drinking session in Alice Springs.

Through tender coaxing, they learned that the girl's name was Moira and as far as he could ascertain, she actually came from Numbulwar in Eastern Arnhem Land. Numbulwar is located on the western coast of the Gulf of Carpentaria at the mouth of the Rose River. Moira and her sister, Sue, had travelled to Alice Springs to go to a camp but as so often will happen, had melted into the seedy side of town living. The women fussed over her and the shy and withdrawn Moira seemed embarrassed at all the attention. Bill knew his small protected family had just had a reality check on the dangers of the outside world.

Moira initially moved in with Bill, Nala and Arora but after only a week and with her health greatly improved, quietly moved into Magnu's caravan. He and Balun had obtained small vans when the family had taken over the new grader purchased from an old friend of Bill's. Bill nodded in agreement; his little tribe was expanding yearly and on a subsequent trip into Alice Springs, Magnu and Moira returned with her sister, Sue, also dishevelled and thin. The family rallied together and once Sue had been cleaned up, to everyone's delight she joined Balun in *his* caravan. The two newcomers slotted in to their new family environment. Balun and Magnu had learnt well from Bill and Wayne and treated their new women with dignity and care.

Three years passed and the camp site of the Strong family became a familiar sight all over isolated Northern Territory.

In town, they had slowly integrated and been accepted but while they stayed in town a few weeks each season, their preference was the bush where they lived and worked together.

Wayne and his girls produced five children; Jumi was the first to give birth to a boy and Akala to two bouncing baby girls. Younga gave birth to a boy and girl, and to everyone's surprise, Arora gave birth to a baby girl! Bill became a proud father for the second time.

Every birth in the hospital was recorded and the records of each delivery were passed on to hospital workers. They in turn then applied and arranged for government workers to supply benefits to all of the women, including child endowment and other necessary provisions that are available to all Australians.

Bill was surprised at how easy it all was; no doubt facilitated by the ease with which authority accepted the paperwork and no doubt used to the often inability to document Aboriginal Australians. Bill and Arora, who went by the name Arora Strong, registered the birth of their daughter Margaret Strong without any probing or questioning. At last the family was legal.

Two more seasons went by and the family thrived. The children played happily and safely, guarded by seven women all sharing the child-raising duties and the men's business flourished. Wayne finished his modest home adding two more rooms for his growing family; Magnu and Balun, with the help of their extended family built two units on the land and they both now had pregnant wives.

One evening, Nala, the contented matriarch, was watching television when she saw a segment on La Grange Mission in Western Australia, now called Bidgydanga. Tears fell down her gentle face as she pointed excitedly to Bill. 'My parents went to that place from the desert with missionary people long time ago.'

Bill's heart thumped as it dawned on him what an idiot he'd been and why he hadn't thought of it before.

'Nala, *I'm* going to take you to that place to hopefully, see your parents,' he told her.

Nala looked at him in astonishment, 'You take me home for visit?'

Bill picked up the tiny figure he loved so much, 'Yes Nala, we will go next week, I promise.'

And with that, Bill picked up the phone and rang a travel agent in Alice Springs.

'Can I book two tickets to Broome please? I'll need accommodation for a week and a hire car. Can you arrange that please?' he boomed with purpose in his voice.

Nala was initially hesitant about flying. She had seen the planes fly far above in the sky but as always, Bill and Arora – who did not want to go – assured the nervous Nala that all would be fine. Nala also knew that her Bill would look after her as he had done from day one. He was her rock and Nala trusted him implicitly.

Life had been good for Bill Strong; business had

boomed since they'd expanded and now he was content and comfortable. It was at that precise moment that he decided on two courses he had to take to bring closure to his life.

ELEVEN

The locals had by now accepted the burgeoning Strong family and no one took any notice apart from tourists who stared curiously as Bill and Nala boarded a flight to Broome. The whole family was there waving madly and happily while trying to placate the screeching children.

Bill gave Arora a big hug and a kiss. He felt a twinge of sadness; it would be their first time away from each other. He had even slept in a chair next to her bed after the birth of Margaret but Bill was now on a mission and had to keep focus. Nala sat upright in her seat with Bill holding her tiny hand tightly, as the plane roared and shuddered down the runway. Bill didn't dare admit to Nala that this flight was *his* first plane ride! He'd never left the Northern Territory before in his life.

Trying to assume the role of the experienced one to placate the nervous Nala, Bill was actually shitting himself.

Looking out of the window he nearly collapsed with shock; his highest vision before had been from the grader. The little hand he was holding was unwittingly supporting him.

Too tense and uptight, they declined any offer of food or drink on the flight and were both relieved when the plane eventually screamed to a bumpy halt in Broome. Picking up their luggage, they went directly to the hire car company and set off to their hotel. Bill knew how to use a GPS so with much concentration, they followed the "voice" in this new and foreign land; it was all so different.

Bill suggested they rest that afternoon and then go clothes shopping before driving the one hundred and eight kilometres to Bidgy, as it was known, in the morning. Bill so wanted the trip to be a memorable one for Nala; she was his true love and had been such a loyal and good companion in all the time he had known her. After afternoon tea, Bill insisted on buying Nala some new clothes. He enjoyed being there while she tried on each different outfit, nodding with approval and revelling in her blatant joy. Nala had come such a long way in her life. Jarra had deliberately kept her isolated for all those years and now here she was, parading her new clothes in an air-conditioned shop. Tiny Nala beamed with pride as her Bill spoiled her with gifts. Nala left the shopping centre wearing a beautiful sarong, pretty sandals and colourful jewellery adorning her dainty neck. No one present would have even considered that several years back, this poised and elegant-looking woman had been wandering the desert naked.

Nala and Bill were booked into one of the best hotels in Broome. Bill wanted to show Nala just how much he appreciated her love and support and wanted nothing but the best for her; he even trimmed his beard!

After they'd unpacked in their luxurious room, they shared a shower and fell onto the huge bed laughing. Nala draped her slim legs around Bill as they lunged at each other madly and passionately before falling apart and dozing off. It had been a good day. That evening, Bill phoned room service and ordered a meal; two large steaks washed down with a sweet wine. This was a special occasion.

Nala awoke early, keen to start the day and shook Bill hurriedly. She could not wait to see her parents again after decades. During their trip, Nala told Bill how her family had come in from the desert at the instructions from missionaries at La Grange, a Catholic Mission.

Passing the Port Smith turn-off, Bill knew they were nearly there. Nala became more restless and fidgety with each kilometre and Bill smiled as he looked at her. What a surprise her parents will get when they see this stunning woman. Gone is the little girl who left their camp with her "promised" husband.

Bill eventually pulled up at an office and made enquiries about Nala's parents. She had no idea if they were still alive or had even moved. Nala was saddened to learn that her father had died but yes, her mother was still alive and lived in a small house on her own at the back of town. After getting directions, Bill drove Nala to the street and after a short search, found what they thought and hoped was the house. They knocked on the door and waited. Then they heard footsteps approaching.

As it opened, Bill knew immediately that they had found Nala's mother. There was a strong Afghan influence and to Bill's surprise and Nala's delight, appeared to be in good health and younger than he had imagined.

The lady peered at Nala for a few minutes and then slowly, recognition began to spread across her face. She let out a great cry and wailed her daughter's name. After all these years, they knew immediately who each other was. Even tough old Bill was choked as he witnessed the women embrace each other, sobbing with joy. But Bill knew now that he had one other matter to attend to upon his return.

All that day, mother and daughter sat holding hands and exchanging stories. Nala learnt that Lara, her mother, was her last living relative as her father and two brothers had died due to accidents and ill health. Nala talked constantly, telling her mother all about her life and as Bill watched them, he knew what he had to do. There was no way he would leave Lara here on her own. He caught Nala's attention and exercised his power as head of his now large family. 'Nala, we'll pack your mum's bags and bring her back home to our place where she belongs. She needs to be with family.'

The expressions on their faces said it all. Loneliness had played a big part of Lara's life and now she suddenly had family and plenty of them by Nala's accounts. Only seven hours after arriving, Bill found himself back in the Bidgy office, advising them that Lara's house was vacant and would be available for occupancy as she was moving to Alice Springs.

The home Lara had lived in was badly in need of repair; taps didn't work, her stove was broken and over the years, it had gradually deteriorated into a hovel. Lara had been in despair, alone and had no one to turn to for help.

Bill and Nala didn't inform the hotel that they were bringing back an "extra" guest. After buying her some new clothes, they managed to sneak Lara into their room. Once Lara had showered and was dressed, Bill and Nala hid her in the bathroom when the evening meal was delivered. Phoning the airline, Bill changed the flight to the following morning as he was anxious to get home. They had both achieved what they had come for and missed home desperately.

As per normal, Bill spent the night with two women. Nala snuggled next to him as her mother lay on the edge of the bed. They talked for hours. Lara was overjoyed at the sudden change in her life and could not believe all that was taking place.

Their flight home was still nerve-racking but Bill overcame his fear by feeling immensely proud of what he had accomplished. To be bringing back Nala's mother was enormous! The whole Strong mob was waiting anxiously at the airport and one would have thought they had been gone months; such was the laughter, hugging and kissing all round. That evening a huge feast was cooked as Lara sat like a queen among her newly extended family. She was now their grandmother and she certainly excelled from day one in her new role.

Wayne was really happy to have his father home; he had been missed by everyone, especially Arora who had moped about watching the road for their return.

Bill and Wayne, who had spent so many quiet years together, now sat surveying the scene of chaos before them. Bill cuddled his precious daughter and his chest filled with fatherly pride. But a frown crossed his wrinkled forehead as he knew that there was one more goal outstanding. Arora came and sat next to him and taking her hand he bent slightly towards her and kissed her. Arora placed her head on his shoulder as she watched her children and grandchildren playing and laughing. She was at peace.

TWELVE

For some weeks, unbeknownst to the others, Bill had been doing some research. He was trying to find the address of Sarah Andrews. Bill was on a quest. Nala had found her mother which was just wonderful but for years now, Bill had been mulling over an issue that tore him apart and he did not know whether to seek answers or let sleeping dogs lie.

So concerned had he become that he eventually confided in Wayne. Wayne thought it over for a few days and agreed with his father that Arora had a right to know her true heritage; their main concern was Nala – she still believed Arora was *her* daughter. *What would such a revelation do to her?* They both loved her immensely. But as Bill pointed out to Wayne, *Nala had found her mother; did Arora not have the same right?*

Bill hired a private detective agency to locate Sarah and the investigative agency came back within twenty-four hours. Yes, they had found her living in America and she had remarried. *Now what to do*, Bill asked himself. With the name and address now in his sweaty hands, Bill knew the letter he was to write was the most important document he would ever write. In fact, he was totally unskilled and of course inexperienced with having to deal with such a daunting task, that the burden hung heavily over him like a black cloud.

For several nights he drafted many letters and then ripped them up until seven days later, looking weary and drained, he re-read his final draft and felt satisfied. He put it in an envelope and the following morning, while the girls shopped, walked to the post office and posted it. He should have felt relief but doubts began to plague him and he prayed that the outcome would be a positive one but he also knew that his keeping it all to himself was selfish and immoral.

When Bill returned home, everybody was preparing for another trip; this time the men had a contract west of Alice Springs. Usually Bill was thrilled at the start of a new season but despite the enthusiasm, he felt a strong sense of despair and doubt rising within, like a volcano about to erupt.

It must have been a strange sight when the long convoy of graders, trucks, caravans and vehicles lined up ready for an early departure. Dogs ran about barking, children shrieked and yelped with happiness! Bill didn't think there would be much sleep that night. The dogs would accompany them on their trip but in their absence, their ponies were going to be looked after by a female doctor who had built a home on acreage next door.

Retiring early, Bill woke with a start, his heart racing and his skin clammy. A cold sweat covered his body as he recalled the most terrible nightmare. Arora was being dragged away by police as a shattered Nala stood looking at him, devastated and betrayed. The small bedside light was on and Arora was breastfeeding Margaret. Although she was two years old, it was the practice of nomads to breastfeed for many years because the young ones took a while to digest bush food and then of course, their dependence on food availability.

Bill went straight to the bathroom, washing his face in

icy cold water and gasping for breath. Again, a sense of foreboding came over him. *What had he done!* His soul felt heavy.

Bill Strong was a simple man; raised by an Auntie who drank too much and an Uncle who beat him relentlessly for any perceived indiscretion. Bill's lifelong desire had been to provide for those he loved with the opportunity to enjoy family life – something he had so desperately screamed for during his young life.

He shut the bathroom door and sat on the toilet seat, sobbing. If he were to lose his family now, it would destroy him. Meeting Nala and Arora had given him something he had always yearned for; a loving family. Bill was in his element surrounded by them and he would actually give his life in a blink for his daughter Margaret. The sun rose each morning for him when he held her in his arms each day before going out to work. His very being was consumed by her and the two women whom he loved more than life itself.

The sun streaked through the window and he knew he *must* be strong and go on. He had made the decision and knew that had he not followed that particular path, the issue of Arora would have haunted him forever. Hiding such a secret would have been morally wrong.

He left the bathroom and went into the kitchen, trying to put on a brave face as Arora and Nala looked at him with concern. Bill had not been with either of them for the last five nights. He grinned sheepishly as he patted them both on the bottoms and scooped up Margaret.

'Too much eating last night, bit crook eh,' patting his belly sheepishly.

Everyone apart from Nala and her mother had some sort of vehicle to drive as the convoy snaked its way onto the highway heading north. It was going to be a long day; the caravans and trucks would arrive at the overnight stay first. Balun and Magnu would come in late with the two graders. Wayne had planned the journey which would take four days to reach the camp spot. He had picked out an area next to a small stream which still held water in several clear pools. The children would be able to swim and play while the women would sit on the banks watching them. Moira had been educated and each day she spent time teaching the children the basics of education. Although three of the children had now reached school age, the family had chosen to home school them. Bill and Wayne wanted to maintain their lifestyle and hoped, as the siblings grew older, that they would enter the family business. In Bill's simplistic view on life, despite their limited education, they had done "alright". Many of the kids around Alice left school at sixteen and never got a job. The two men hoped to guide the younger generation into keeping the family tradition going; they had the freedom of the road and theirs was a happy lifestyle.

Setting up camp again was the usual chaos; dogs yapping, kids yelling and getting in the way, the women's high-pitched screams piercing the hot air. Bill looked at the scene before him and his heart ached even more at the possibility of the fallout from his actions. Suddenly, he felt old and inadequate. He never ever wanted to hurt anyone, only love them.

At twilight, the two graders turned up. Tomorrow Bill would set up road signs – now a new rule – and work would commence.

It was a month-long job and lucrative, the usual

contractor on this section had taken work closer to Darwin and the authorities had offered Bill and his gang a good contract to repair the road. Bill only found out before he left that in fact, a mine was to open in the area and so now understood why the money was so good. Indigenous communities did not usually get such treatment as certain funding was allocated each season and that was it. Bill understood why; there were no tax returns or income stream from Indigenous settlement so mining revenue was a welcome money source for both state and federal governments.

The following morning two of the girls set off placing the road signs while loaders unloaded fuel, spares and supplies from the trucks. They then started to fill the trucks with gravel and the excavator began to clean out drains that the floods had blocked. To his great relief, as soon as Bill started grading, the concentration took his mind, albeit briefly, off his black thoughts. Indeed, it was great to be back at work and this was his favourite time of year. Everyone had their own little job and routine. The women's duties varied from washing, minding the children or preparing meals. Since the girls had learnt to drive, midday meals were now delivered and Bill would sit with Arora under a shady tree eating the lunch she had prepared. He reflected how, in the past, sitting beneath a clear, blue sky, they would make love but sadly he had lost his sex drive; the stress of the unknown regarding his letter had affected him badly.

He also knew that Nala and Arora missed the intimacy; he saw the disappointment and sadness in their eyes as he was sure they thought he no longer wanted them but this was far from the case and this only added to his woes.

THIRTEEN

Sarah Brown sat at the kitchen bench in her condo which overlooked the river. She had lived in America now for many years; married to a man she had met two years after her separation and decision to move to America.

The past still impacted on her even after all this time. Danny, her husband, had gone off to work. They ran a small business in town and Sarah often helped out but today she had decided to stay home and catch up with a few personal chores and then relax. Business had slowed due to the economic downturn but thankfully it had not affected them and they were quite comfortable, even contemplating selling up within the next couple of years to retire.

Sipping her coffee, she saw the postman deliver mail. Normally Sarah waited until the end of the day but for some reason she decided to go downstairs and collect it.

If there was anything of interest to read, she could enjoy it with her coffee – solitude and peace – bliss.

Picking up the mail she returned to her seat and sorted out the bills and annoying brochures but one envelope stood out amongst all of them. She noticed the postmark; Alice Springs. Her heart began to thump in her chest as she picked up a knife to open it. As she began to read, she found she could not breathe and began to shake uncontrollably. Surely, after all these years, no one would be so vicious as to send a hoax letter, although as she read it, she knew that the writer was genuine. It read,

Dear Sarah,

I write this letter after much anguish and soul searching. Please forgive my writing as I am not that well educated but I sincerely believe I am a good person.

How to start. Believe me, I have spent many nights thinking on the matter but I have to inform you that I honestly believe I am living with your daughter Mary who I confess I love unconditionally. The story of how our relationship transpired is one of almost unbelievable circumstances and I will try and relay it to you to the best of my ability.

I am a grader driver and contractor repairing roads mainly to isolated Indigenous communities. Several years ago, about two hundred kilometres west of Ayers Rock, I was grading a road unknown to me when I came across two houses. Sitting at the camp fire was a small woman. As it was lunchtime, I stopped for lunch and invited her to share my meagre offering. I noted at the time she was naked and had no food other than bush tucker. As I speak the local dialect she understood my questions and she informed me that she had come from the west, and I remember her pointing in the direction of her country. Nothing exists between here and west Australia but desert and wild country. When she eventually relaxed, the woman who I now live with, called Nala, called out to others. I had not noticed them hiding behind desert bush. To my shock, a white woman and five young half-castes approached.

Over time I have gleaned from Nala, who at the time had lost her husband Jarra, as had Arora, whom I believe is *your* daughter. They lived a nomadic life with Jarra who had only died that season. The whole group wore no clothes and their condition was indicative of bush nomads.

My information from Nala is that she gave birth to a child at the time of Mary's disappearance at Ayers Rock. It appears the baby was born dead and Jarra removed the dead child while Nala was semi-conscious. She had experienced a terribly, painful delivery. That evening, confused and disorientated, Nala heard a baby crying and I think and firmly believe that she picked up Mary from your tent and simply walked off into the desert.

Nala and her mob had only been at the area for a few days. She then left the area with her lover Jarra and they returned to their homeland range. Arora was raised with them and in time, Jarra fathered five children with her.

I have agonised over the whole sad matter, but may

never have peace if at least I did not have the fortitude to inform you. My nightmare is that I will now lose my family whom I love more than life itself but you have a right to know and perhaps your life may have closure.

I send you this letter heavy in heart and sincerely hope I have done the right thing.

Yours sincerely

Bill Strong

Alice Springs

NT

She read it over and over again. It all sounded so bizarre but then it dawned on her that her whole life had been ruined. The burden of being convicted and jailed for something she did not do had obviously taken a terrible toll on her mentally, emotionally and physically. She also knew that despite the new evidence that a dingo had indeed taken her baby, within the eyes of the public, she was still guilty. In shocked silence, Sarah sat quietly contemplating her next move. She knew she had to visit the Strong family and from there she would play it by ear. The anguish of the writer was authentic and she knew that this person loved Arora who could be, above all odds, her daughter Mary.

But Sarah also knew that if the press even got a whiff of this again, their lives would be destroyed for a second time. She had learnt the hard way that man's inhumanity to man knows no boundaries.

That evening she discussed the matter with her husband who, like her, was convinced the letter was real and the fear he held for Mary, should things become public. It was agreed that only Sarah would make the journey. To try and avoid discovery, she dyed her hair and bought large sunglasses. She organised the plane tickets for a journey that she knew, in spite of all that she had endured, could possibly be the most soul-destroying discovery yet, if only, she prayed, if only.

Using her American passport she applied for a visa and hoped no leak would come from immigration about her impending visit. All was calm as she nervously waved goodbye to her husband; bound back to Australia and the nightmare she had buried in her mind but one that resurfaced many times in her darkest moments.

Arriving in Sydney, Sarah stayed at the airport motel ready to catch the plane the following morning to Alice Springs and hopefully, closure. She didn't know what to expect nor what her reaction would be but all she knew was that she had no choice but to make the trip.

As the plane landed at Alice Springs airport, old and distasteful memories flooded back and she hurriedly picked up the hire car, drove out of the airport to the address in the letter. Bill had not included a phone number. When she located the address she looked at the cluster of houses and wondered about the life her precious daughter had led in this harsh desert with her family. Tears welled in her eyes and she choked back sobs. Disappointed, Sarah found no one at home; the place was locked and as she was about to leave, a car pulled up and a middle-aged lady stepped out.

'Next door neighbour! And pony carer,' she yelled to Sarah.

'Old friend of Bill, come to visit from Darwin,' Sarah replied.

'Bill and his mob are camped at a spring on the springs track. I've a map, I'll show you,' Dr Cynthia Dare cheerfully replied. 'Just like bloody old Bill not to tell you, hell, with his mob, it's a wonder he remembers what day it is.'

'My fault, I never told him I was coming, knew him years ago when I worked here,' said Sarah nonchalantly.

'What did you work at?' Dr Dare shot back.

'In the courts,' Sarah replied thinking quickly.

'That would have been interesting,' Dr Dare replied laying out a map.

'Oh I see your hire car has a GPS; that'll show you the track. Just drive until you see a large camp of women, kids and dogs; that'll be Bill and his mob.'

Returning to town Sarah bought a few supplies as she had worked out it was at least a two-day drive to the camp. She was glad she'd hired the car for ten days just in case of such an eventuality. Sarah began to feel paranoid that she would be recognised. Refuelling she wore a scarf, paid as quickly as possible and drove off. She drove until midnight, eventually turning off the highway on the springs track. She was tired and pulled off the road but slept erratically until dawn before continuing. Her expectation and nerves fumbled around inside her violently, making her feel slightly nauseous.

Sipping occasionally from a water bottle, Sarah lowered the sun shade as the heat danced off the landscape. The land was devoid of life in the merciless midday sun. Glancing at her watch she saw that she had been driving straight for eight hours. Wondering whether to stop at the next resting spot, Sarah's breath was taken away as she rounded the corner. There before her was a large group of caravans, fuel trailers and several Aboriginal women moving around slowly. As she pulled in she noticed children and dogs splashing in the water below. Her heart skipped a beat as there, seated cross-legged on the bank with two other women, was a white woman with blonde sun-bleached hair. Sarah needed no blood test; the features and face convinced her immediately that she was staring at her daughter Mary. There was no doubt.

As she stepped out of the car a young Aboriginal woman approached her. In a trembling voice, Sarah said,

'Hi, I'm Sarah, a friend of Bill's. Is he here?'

Moira replied, 'Bill, him out working, he come home maybe later.'

'Can I wait? I am very tired,' replied Sarah, her heart racing.

'No problem, perhaps you sit under tree in shade with Nala and Arora, wait longa there,' Moira replied pointing in their direction.

Sarah walked up to the women who were watching her with caution.

'Hi, my name is Sarah and I've come to visit my old friend Bill,' she said, her voice breaking.

'You sit here, then perhaps Bill he come soon,' Nala told her gently.

Sarah sat down next to the women taking in the scene before her. She was unable to stop herself from staring at Arora, finding it hard to comprehend that here before her, was the daughter she long thought dead. Now she was unable to even picture her as a baby, yet oddly, she felt as though she had come home. Watching the women and the camp movement, Sarah recognised just how happy and uncomplicated Arora's life was; a world of innocence and so far removed from the savage reality of the modern world. This man, Bill Strong, who had sheltered these people, certainly was a rare breed. Sarah began to relax. She was worn out and felt herself dozing while embracing the wonderful sounds of children, dogs and the women's laughter. Some of the younger ones joined the children in the cool water below. Sarah seemed to be accepted, perhaps not like she had envisaged but then foolishly reminded herself that she was a stranger *not* a member of the family. Snapping herself out of the state she was in, Sarah walked into the clear water and seeing Margaret paddling, picked her up and wondered who here was her own blood. The whole situation seemed surreal when she thought about all her suffering and agony.

Looking around her, Sarah understood Bill's anxiety and concern. He did not want to change anything about the situation of these carefree, happy people.

Sarah then knew that she could not and would not, alter the course of these people's lives. Their world was so different to what she had initially envisaged. They focused on family bonding, support for each other and were so far removed from the "real" world. Their lives were wonderfully simple and yet fragile. She knew then, as she stood holding her granddaughter, that to change the status quo would destroy too many lives. A tear trickled down her cheek as she gave the infant a hug and returned her to her mother. Sarah suddenly felt old and weary but incredibly happy. Her daughter was alive and happy, living within an intimate family unit with six children and grandchildren and leading a life without complication and protected by a man who, despite his unusual living arrangements, was a man with high morals and soul.

The afternoon wore on as Sarah gleaned more and more about their lives, particularly that of Arora's. These women needed and loved their men. Their ability to share the love of one man and live peacefully and in harmony certainly would not work in the world Sarah inhabited. She envied their ignorance of another society where treachery and greed walked hand in hand. Here, in the bush, these women lived in paradise. Sarah then learned that three of her granddaughters lived with Bill's son, yet somehow, watching the three younger women and the partners of her grandsons, she felt it all seemed *so natural*. The so-called puritans would frown upon it all, feigning disgust and horror but it was blatantly obvious to Sarah that everyone in the camp was loved and respected. There was nothing to suspect otherwise.

Bill was the first one to return home that evening as he had been feeling unwell. There was a burning pain in his chest, no doubt due to the stress of his actions and the unknown repercussions. His health was being impacted. He didn't see the car or Sarah until he went over to the group of women. Arora, smiling, brought their daughter to him, as was his first task every night when he came home from work and then, as he noticed Sarah, a look of alarm spread over his features.

Picking up his daughter, he gave her a special hug as he approached Sarah who stood holding her hand out to him.

Sarah saw the look of agony on his face; she also noted the kindness in his troubled look.

'Hi Bill, remember me? Sarah Brown!' She then leaned in towards him quickly and whispered, 'Bill, please calm down, no one here knows who I am and *never* will.'

Bill felt as though the weight had been lifted from his shoulders.

'Sorry Sarah, my whole world has been turned upside down since I wrote to you,' he replied quietly.

'Bill, my dear man, do you *really* think I would destroy the lives of all these beautiful people. I even forgive little Nala. The past is the past and my daughter died a long time ago; we are all living in different times,' said Sarah as they walked along the riverbank out of earshot.

'Thank you Sarah, thank you. Can you imagine the media storm if this got out?' Bill said, shaking his head at the prospect.

'In my wildest dreams, I'd *never* wish that on my worst enemy Bill. There's no need for blood tests, Arora is of my blood and I gave birth to her and to make sure she keeps living her life without reserve, I set her free. I know you will always take care of her and, well, can I visit sometimes and stay a couple of days, just to watch them all grow into adults?' Sarah asked, tears running into her mouth.

'Sarah, I give you my word. Our place will always be yours. We will both die with this secret as I was fearful no good would come of it. If the story were exposed, too many would suffer,' Bill replied gravely.

'Bill, with your permission, may I stay and play with my family perhaps for a couple of days? I feel like you, old and tired. My life has suffered; too much stress.'

Then Sarah chuckled and looking at Bill said, 'For once Bill *I* have won! Fuck the media!'

Bill chuckled too; he liked Sarah. How strong was she to have endured so much and yet she remained brave and positive.

Having bared their souls, the two returned to the camp and Bill told Arora and Nala that Sarah would be staying for a couple of nights. A spare bunk was made up in Bill's caravan. Sarah had become a member of the mob and joined in all the camp activities including taking the midday meal out to Bill and the boys. She could not believe how much she loved it all and to be able to share the lives of her family would go down as one of her most cherished experiences.

FOURTEEN

Three glorious days soon passed for Sarah but in her heart she knew she would eventually have to return to her world. Many times when she found herself seated next to Arora, she could not resist reaching out to her and when she looked into her eyes, it gave her the strength and resolve to move forward with her life. Arora and her children would forever be in her heart.

With tears and her heart crying out, Sarah hugged everyone as she prepared to leave. Bill had tears streaming down his face as the car pulled out heading back to Alice then on to Sydney and home to America. Sarah obviously had mixed emotions leaving her darling daughter; she never wanted to leave her but knew that her daughter lived a unique, happy life and she certainly would not consider doing anything to change it. She may have lived as a nomad all these years but under the watchful and loving eye of Bill Strong, Sarah knew that Arora and the rest of the mob would be well taken care of and more importantly, loved and respected. Yep, he was one helluva man.

With Sarah gone and the status quo uninterrupted, all of Bill's anxiety left him. Contentment returned and everyone went back to their routine and life continued in its own special way. Bill returned to work a lighter man but he could not get Sarah out of his mind and how wrongfully the media had manipulated the story for their benefit. *How easily is public perception influenced by the hungry, vicious press.*

Catching up with Wayne, Bill stopped for lunch. They sat under a tree, gazing into the distance while they ate and chatted.

'I'm so glad that it all turned out okay Dad. Gee, I was worried about you and I know Arora and Nala are *still* worried. I gather from the girls' chatter that things are a bit slow in the bed mate,' chuckled Wayne nudging him in the ribs with his elbow.

'Cheeky bugger. Yep, to be honest I've been so stressed I'm finding it hard to get going again. Once upon a time', grinned Bill, 'lust was uncontrollable; now I can't seem to get fired up.'

'Listen Dad, tonight I'm going to give you a Viagra, that'll help. I can go all night with them,' Wayne laughed boastfully.

'Bloody Viagra! What's that?' shot back Bill.

'Dad honestly, sometimes you should *really* listen to the news. Viagra is a tablet that gets you, well, you know, up,' Wayne replied getting up to head back to work. 'You are definitely having one tonight.'

Bill forgot about their conversation and started his grader up. Boy, was he relieved that the whole episode was over and he was back to doing the work he loved without any distractions.

That evening, Arora turned up to collect him and she had really tried hard to look attractive for him. She wore a short dress and had a bow in her hair. When Bill saw her, he knew that he would be able to make love to her. His anxiety had gone and he tried to relax.

Wayne arrived home being driven by the cheeky Jumi. When Wayne spotted his father sitting having a cold drink, he went over to him and said smiling, 'Here Dad, take this and see what happens.'

'What's that?' asked Bill as he looked at the small blue pill.

'Bloody Viagra Dad! I told you!' Wayne whispered strongly as he walked off.

Bill looked at the tablet. Now Bill was not a man to take tablets. He shook his head and swallowed it; not giving it another thought.

After showering, Bill ate his tea prepared by the girls and as darkness came over the land he undressed and went to bed. The air was hot and sticky so he lay back on his bed naked. Nala and Arora had always slept naked and over the years Bill had got into the habit too.

As he lay there in the humid condition, his thoughts turned to the girls and how much he had missed the intimacy. With that, he felt some movement and looked in awe at his upright rock hard penis. He could hear Nala pottering around in the van and softly called her in. What greeted her was a thick, throbbing cock. She smiled, dropped her dress and mounted.

Nala bucked fervidly as Bill glanced down at his shining wet member pounding in and out. Never before had he lasted so long and grabbing Nala's small buttocks, he rammed deeper into her. Small groans escaped her as they picked up the tempo in pure lust until they reached a crescendo. Their spent bodies were covered in sweat. Bill had never experienced such an exquisite ejaculation.

As Bill's breathing returned to normal he heard Arora come in and to his surprise and absolute delight, his member rose to the occasion. Arora sat on the side of the bed and slowly removed her ribbon from her hair. Bill sat up and turned to glance at the snoring, Nala. The smell of sex filled the air as he pulled Arora down; she looked wild-eyed as he turned and mounted her. Bill had always been good with sex but now he rode her like a man possessed, bringing her to orgasm again and again. The sweat dripped from him as he drove into her wet valley lustfully. The bed rocked as they bounced up and down until their bodies opened up and climaxed. Bill moaned as once again, he felt the flood unload.

When Bill rolled off, he was amazed to see that he was still stiff and that it took some time for him to relax and be flaccid again.

Nala and Arora slept soundly and as Bill lay next to them, he mused, *Yep, it sure was good to be back to normal.* Before he drifted off though, he'd already planned to take the girls for a little trip into the Alice the next day and while there, Bill thought he might pay the doc a visit to get a few more Viagra.